The Jew Girls Adventure Series
Book One

You Can Call Me Andy

Jess Brady

Carla Perry

S. L. Heumer

The Jew Girls Adventure Series
Book One

You Can Call Me Andy

Bubbelah Press
an imprint of
Dancing Moon Press

The Jew Girls Adventure Series Book One:
You Can Call Me Andy
Copyright © 2022 Jess Bondy, Sara Heimlich, and Carla Perry

Publisher's Note: This is a work of fiction.

Without limiting the rights under copyright reserved above, no part of this publication may be reproduced, stored in, or introduced into a retrieval system, or transmitted in any form or by any means (electronic, mechanical, photocopying, recording, or otherwise) without the prior written permission of the authors, except in the case of brief quotations or sample images embedded in critical articles or reviews. The scanning, uploading, and distribution of any part of this book via the Internet, or any other means without the permission of the authors is illegal and punishable by law. Please purchase only authorized editions and do not participate in or encourage electronic piracy of copyrightable materials. Your support of the authors' rights is appreciated. For permission, address your inquiry to: BubbelahPress@gmail.com

Paperback ISBN: 978-1-945587-80-1
Library of Congress Control Number: 2022943524

The Jew Girls
The Jew Girls Adventure Series Book One: You Can Call Me Andy
1. Jews; 2. Jew Girls; 3. Adventure; 4. Jewish holidays; 5. Purim;
6. Hamantaschen; 7. Glossary of Yiddish & Hawaiian words; 8. Maui
9. Newport, Oregon; 10. Solar energy; I. TITLE

Book inspired and drafted by *Carla Perry*
Book editing, design, and project production: *Carla Perry*
Hamantaschen illustration in Appendix C: *Sara Heimlich*
Cover design, cover production: *Sarah Gayle Art*
Manufactured in the United States of America

Bubbelah Press
   an imprint of Dancing Moon Press
P.O. Box 832, Newport, OR 97365
Phone: 541-574-7708
BubbelahPress@gmail.com

FIRST EDITION

Dedication

With great appreciation for our researcher and dog wrangler.

The Jew Girls are totally grateful to our community
for all the support you've provided
during this creative writing process.
A sheynem dank, y'all.

Which means:
Thank you so very much!

Especially to our "first readers"
who read numerous drafts and provided vital feedback.

Contents

Chapter 1: The Adventure Begins 9
Chapter 2: Who's Lying Now? 14
Chapter 3: Last Call For Maui 28
Chapter 4: Coffee Ready Yet? 31
Chapter 5: Stylin' By The Surf 36
Chapter 6: Hangovers Don't Fib 43
Chapter 7: The Road To Hell Isn't Paved At All 50
Chapter 8: There Be Dancin' Tonight! A Purim Interlude 58
Chapter 9: No Time To Shoot The Shit 65
Chapter 10: Break In! 69
Chapter 11: What The Hell Just Happened? 79
Chapter 12: Filthy-Rich Dreams 91
Chapter 13: Millions Of Oxy Night Rides 98
Chapter 14: The Liar's Downfall 107
Chapter 15: Words Like That 114
Chapter 16: Not Quite The Ending 118
Chapter 17: What Does The Iguana Say? 120
Appendix A: Yiddish & Hawaiian Words 131
Appendix B: The Story Of Purim 133
Appendix C: Hamantaschen Pastry Recipe 136
Appendix D: Real Musicians Mentioned In This Story 138
About the Authors 141

Chapter 1: The Adventure Begins

"Luba says she has a tummy ache and so won't be joining us," says Lindy as she sets down her phone and exhales a cloud of smoke. "I should believe her, but something was off in her voice." Lindy takes another deep, long inhale of her cigarette.

Lindy is short and trim. Her hair is a meticulous russet brown. Vintage sparkling jewelry jangles at her wrists, ears, and throat. She's in her mid-somethings, same as her two best friends, Zoey and Luba. The three have known each other since vying for the last of the shredded beets at the Oceana Food Coop salad bar.

"That's all Luba said?" asks Zoey.

It's late afternoon. The rain is relentless and the sky is so dark that the lamps are already on. It's a typical winter day on the Central Oregon Coast. Lindy and Zoey are in the living room of Lindy's tidy, upscale, second-floor condo at the north end of Newport. The place is jam-packed with antiques and fine art, but the soaring ceilings and enormous windows facing the ocean make it seem uncluttered.

The Jew Girls Adventure Series

The two have already shared a joint and munched on several apricot-filled, gluten-free hamantaschen pastries stacked on a silver tray, close at hand. Their coffee mugs are empty. The rain, the early darkness, and undoubtedly the cannabis contribute to their inertia.

Zoey's dog Andy, a German shepherd/collie rescue, sits nearby. His eyes are on the triangle-shaped pastries.

Luba's phone call had interrupted their cozy indolence.

"Well, *bubbelah*," says Lindy to Zoey, her thoughts immediately drifting off in another direction. After a long pause, Lindy refocuses and says, "*Oy gevalt*, what was your question?"

"I asked if Luba said anything else," says Zoey.

Lindy takes another pull on her cigarette, lets out a slow smoky breath, and crushes the stub in an ashtray. Her brow is furrowed. "Oh! I remember. Luba said she needs to lie low for a few days, maybe a week. She said to celebrate Purim without her."

"Well, that makes no sense and that's not gonna happen," says Zoey. "She's the one who insists we celebrate all the major Jewish holidays together."

"Where did I put my damn freakin' cigarettes?" asks Lindy. Traces of her gravelly New York accent remain, especially when foul language erupts from those dainty bronze lips.

"In your left hand," says Zoey, which makes her laugh because sure enough, that's exactly where Lindy's pack of More Menthols is located. "Besides," she continues. "I thought you gave up smoking and were in training for the Newport Marathon."

"Very funny," says Lindy. "The last time I ran for pleasure was when I was a kid and the Good Humor ice cream truck drove off before I could get there."

You Can Call Me Andy

Zoey's cherubic smile is surrounded by the boisterous mass of her unruly auburn curls. She's had her share of bad luck around money and men, but in between all the nastiness, there's been enough downright pleasure to give her eyes their mischievous twinkle and the beginning of delicate laugh lines. Zoey spent most of her young adult years traveling with those various men, and somehow became proficient in Finnish, Urdu, Maori, and Gaelic. Due to the infrequent need for those particular languages, she's proved less than helpful on international stopovers.

"Luba is lying," says Andy the dog, then he stands and inches closer to the hamantaschen. Speaking English is just one of the many skills he's picked up while hanging out with Zoey.

"Maybe it's just another secret she's keeping from us," says Lindy. "Luba thinks all her secrets are secret. Like, what's with that locked bedroom in her apartment? The one with the mirrors and all that tacky ballerina art we're not supposed to know about. Oh, that reminds me... that lock-picking workshop was the best birthday present ever!"

"I thought you might be ready for a new hobby," giggled Zoey. "I just didn't expect you to use those skills to break into Luba's secret room—just to show off."

They both laugh till they snort.

Then their conversation drifts into silence for a minute as they meander through the fog in their brains.

"Wait, what were we just talking about?" asks Lindy.

"Luba and her secrets," says Zoey. "Did you say that secrets aren't lies? But doesn't that depend?"

"Depend on what?" asks Lindy. "What does Andy think?"

"I don't know what Andy thinks," says Zoey. "Ask him yourself."

"Revenge," says Andy as he shifts his body another inch closer to the pastries. His ability to read people is uncanny, even when they're all the way across town.

"I think we should drop in on Luba," says Lindy. "A surprise visit."

Slowly she lights another cigarette with those long, elegant fingers of hers. She checks her cream-colored nails for chipping, and sighs. She flicks the cigarette ash. The stain of bronze lipstick at the end of the More Menthol comforts her. "We could pretend we're concerned about her tummy. Bring her homemade chicken soup. I've got some in the freezer. We don't even need to thaw it."

"Luba will be needing a lot more than chicken soup," says Andy.

"Well, if Luba really is lying to us, it means something serious is going on and you know how much she hates to admit she needs help from her friends," says Lindy. "And if Andy is right, which he always is, then we've got to keep Luba from taking her revenge too far. She may be brilliant and sometimes overly passionate about something or other, but often that gets her in trouble."

"No can do," says Zoey. "I can't visit Luba today because I have to get to City Hall before five o'clock. The County still doesn't want to sell the Fairgrounds, but we need those ten acres for housing and I think I can convince the City to buy back the property."

"Not today," says Lindy. "Friends show up for each other. That's more important."

"I also promised to take Andy down to the Bay Haven this evening," says Zoey. "For the music and dancing. There's a great band playing and Andy's in love with the banjo player."

"Nope," says Lindy. "I repeat, not today. If Luba is lying to us,

You Can Call Me Andy

that's more important. Besides, isn't dancing a deadly sin?"

"Well, revenge for sure is a deadly sin," says Zoey. "Dancing is a virtue. And love is a virtue. But smoking is a vice. You really need to stop smoking, Lindy. Cigarettes are known to cause facial wrinkles."

"I'm trying!" says Lindy as she exhales long and slow.

Lindy stands abruptly. "I'm heading for the kitchen. To get something. What am I getting?"

"Chicken soup?" says Zoey. "And a paper bag for the hamantaschen. We'd better take those with us. You never know."

Chapter 2: Who's Lying Now?

Lindy, Zoey, and Andy the dog arrive at Luba's upscale apartment in the hills east of Newport. Lindy cradles her favorite red leather Coach handbag that contains the Tupperware container of frozen chicken soup. Zoey holds the paper bag of hamantaschen. Andy carries nothing, not even a leash. Lindy knocks on the door. Luba's housekeeper swings the door open.

"Oh no!" the housekeeper says. "You're not supposed to be here."

The two women and the dog rush past the housekeeper and into Luba's home where every room is painted white and has a view of the ocean stretching from the Yaquina Bay Bridge to Yaquina Head. When they reach the threshold of Luba's bedroom, they see a brown Louis Vuitton suitcase on the bed, and Senor Zippy, the iridescent green, ten-pound iguana, resting on Luba's shoulders, sweetly licking her neck. Everything else Luba is wearing is a shade of brown—from her soft leather traveling loafers to the tips of her surprisingly plump fingers.

You Can Call Me Andy

While brown is the only color to be found in her wardrobe, Luba's hair is a severe bottle-black. For all the many years that Lindy and Zoey have known her, Luba has never changed her hairstyle. Bangs sheared off as if someone used a straightedge ruler. The rest twirled up in back in an intricate French braid. She is rail-thin, but with thick piano legs, cherry-red lips, and the bosom of a porn star.

Luba is holding a brown silk caftan, trimmed with gold thread. Other items of clothing are stacked in neat piles. Although she moves quickly to block her friends' view of the suitcase, the effort is futile. The rap hit, "Pimpin," by Megan Thee Stallion, is playing at an ear-splitting volume on Luba's futuristic sound system.

"So, Luba! The truth comes out!" Lindy shouts, trying to be heard over the music. She lights another menthol coffin nail. "Listen," she says, exhaling over her left shoulder. "You don't have a tummy ache! You're going somewhere. Where are you going? How long will you be gone? You're not sick, are you? And please turn down the volume!"

"Stop screaming at me," yells Luba.

"I'm screaming because I can't hear you!" says Lindy.

"I like my music loud!" yells Luba. "If you don't, then leave!"

Zoey puts her hands over her ears. In a calm and soothing, but amplified voice, she says, "We're not going anywhere, Luba. But it's obvious you are."

Luba glares at her friends with the look of cold gefilte fish, which makes the atmosphere stink, but she turns down the volume. It takes a moment for the raucous vibrations to ebb. "Nowhere," Luba says in a much softer voice. "I'm going nowhere. What makes you think I'm not sick?"

The Jew Girls Adventure Series

"Andy told us," Zoey says to Luba.

"Senor Zippy just confirmed it," says Andy, smiling at his iguana friend.

The iguana extends his dewlap—the skin under his neck—in agreement, or alarm, it's hard to tell. But then he licks Luba's neck again as if to emphasize the point.

Andy walks to the bed, pushes the brown garment bag, and grabs Luba's brown toiletry case gently in his teeth. Then he uses his nose to push a tube of suntan lotion until it falls on the floor.

"Suntan lotion?" asks Zoey. "Really, Luba?"

"Yeah, Luba," says Lindy. "Where are you going that requires a caftan and suntan lotion? Do we need a passport?"

A new hip-hop song by Lizzo starts up: *"Mirror, mirror on the wall, Don't say it 'cause I know I'm cute. Blame it on my juice, yeah, blame it on my juice...."*

Lindy sings along for the chorus because she knows the song and can't help herself.

"No, you do NOT need a passport," Luba says, talking over the music until Lindy stops singing. "Neither of you are going anywhere. And I've asked you both to call me by my full name, not just Luba. My name is Luba Vilnitsky."

Lindy and Zoey exchange a look and roll their eyes.

"Sorry, of course. My apologies," says Zoey sarcastically. "But why? Isn't the name Luba distinctive enough?"

"Let's just call it a mystery," says Luba with no humor at all.

"Fine," says Zoey. "But yes we ARE going. We're prepared to leave now, just like you. Andy and I even cancelled our evening plans."

You Can Call Me Andy

"Right," says Lindy. "I get it. She's going to Florida."

"Florida!" repeats Zoey. "Well, my underwear is red, kind of lacy, and it can serve as swimwear too. I travel light. So, Luba, consider me packed and ready."

Everything Zoey is wearing over that racy red underwear was purchased from the Animal Shelter's second-hand store aptly named Pick of the Litter. Her style could be called "disposable casual elegance." She is always ready to travel.

"That's a totally stupid idea," says Luba. "You guys are crazy. What gives you the idea I'm going to Florida?"

"Andy says whatever this is, and wherever you're going, it has to do with revenge," Lindy replies.

"Did someone wrong you?" asks Zoey. "Was it theft? Love gone bad? Betrayal? Are you thinking of doing something criminal and want to keep us in the dark to protect us?"

"Luba, revenge is rarely the best answer," says Lindy.

"Talk to us," says Zoey.

"We can help," says Lindy.

"I think she's planning to fly somewhere," says Zoey.

"Yep," says Lindy looking at the brown suitcase and all that brown clothing on the bed. "The facts do point to that conclusion." Lindy stubs out her cigarette in what could be an ashtray but is really just a decorative white clamshell. "There's no place within a thousand miles of Newport where you'd need suntan lotion. We can get tickets as we board. Don't worry. I brought plenty of credit cards. Luba, does this have to do with cocaine?"

"Luba Vilnitsky is my name!" says Luba. "And no. Absolutely not. You cannot come with me. Both of you, stop asking me questions! What gave you that asinine idea about cocaine?"

The Jew Girls Adventure Series

"It's Florida, for friggin' sake!" says Lindy. "Cocaine is part of everything."

Luba speaks deliberately, enunciating every single word. "I am not going to Florida. And I don't want to talk about it. I don't need your help. You can both leave right now. Take that weird dog with you!"

"Who among us is not weird?" asks Andy, taking no offense.

"If it's not revenge, perhaps she's going there for romance," says Zoey looking curiously at her iguana-topped friend. Then she says, "No, probably not romance."

"Maybe she's going to the Everglades to find a mate for Senor Zippy," says Lindy. "Perhaps the iguana is lonely. He looks lonely there draped over her shoulders. He can see her packing and already misses her. Don't you think so, Zoey? Maybe Senor Zippy wants to go, too. Like a therapy iguana. But there are alligators down there in Florida."

"They capture you," says Zoey. "Take you underneath the surface of the water until you drown. Stuff you into some ragged rock outcropping down in the water and leave you until your flesh begins to decay. Then they eat you. I'm referring to the alligators."

"Dead!" says Lindy.

"Stop it!" says Luba beginning to laugh. "Lindy, I'm not going to the Everglades."

"So," says Lindy. "Is it about a murder in Boca Raton? Oh, my god, Zoey! Boca Raton!"

"Andy was explicit," says Zoey. "He said revenge. Hey, Lindy, you think this has something to do with the espionage case from last year? The one with the Russians."

You Can Call Me Andy

"Don't be silly," says Lindy. "You don't need sunscreen in Russia."

"So it's revenge in Florida!" exclaims Zoey. "Oh, that would be great because I really could use a break from all this rain."

"Maybe she's plotting something despicable," says Lindy. "Oh, Luba Vilnitsky, please take us with you! If it's revenge you intend, count us in."

"What if it requires murder?" Zoey asks Lindy.

"No," Lindy answers. "I draw the line at murder."

"So, there it is, Luba," says Zoey. "No murders. But we need details. And we need them now."

"Yeah," says Lindy. "Why didn't you stop in for Purim cookies and tell us the truth like any friend would? What would it have cost you? A three-minute detour? I made those hamantaschen gluten-free at your request. It's not like you to pull a no-show. So whatever you're hiding and/or denying, snap out of it."

Just then, the housekeeper enters holding a squat crystal glass of Drambuie liqueur and Luba's black cat-eye glasses. She hands both to Luba. "I found these in the freezer again," she says.

"Thank you," says Luba. "I like the coolness wrapped around my temples," she says to her friends.

"About your friends," the housekeeper says as she walks to Luba's closet, "I'm real sorry, ma'am. But I couldn't stop them from entering once the front door was open."

The housekeeper doesn't appear sorry at all as she flips through Luba's brown suits, each one protected by a separate clear garment bag. Down below are Luba's brown, low-heeled pumps in clear shoeboxes. The housekeeper opens a baby-sized garment bag and removes a dark chestnut brown and gold lamé bathing suit.

The Jew Girls Adventure Series

"One more thing," says the housekeeper. "We can't do your nails."

"Why not?" asks Luba. "Am I out of Cinnamon Delight polish?"

"You've run out of time," replies the housekeeper. She surveys the clothes on the bed and the half-filled suitcase. "Oh," she says, and walks back to Luba's closet. She removes a pair of highly polished brown hiking boots. She sets these on a towel on the bed.

Finally, Luba drops her resistance. "*Oy vey*, you people," she says with an exaggerated sigh. "I really do appreciate you bringing the hamantaschen. Can we take them with us? Perhaps we can *nosh* on them on the plane."

"Us?" asks Lindy.

"We're going with you?" asks Zoey. "Cool!"

"Obviously," says Luba. Her friends' tenaciousness has always been a blessing, and a nuisance. "I knew it would turn out this way as soon as you barged in."

"Listen," says Lindy. "I'll call my travel agent to make reservations for three more seats on your flight out of Portland. Zoey, can I borrow your phone? I left mine at home."

Zoey pulls her phone out of her bra and hands it to Lindy.

"To Florida, Luba?" asks Lindy.

"My name is Luba Vilnitsky!" says Luba with exaggerated slowness. "I suppose you do need our destination. It's Maui. But three more seats? There's only two of you."

"I can answer that," says Andy. "Secret Service dogs get their own seat."

Luba nods. "Of course."

You Can Call Me Andy

"Secret Service this time, Andy?" says Zoey. "Really?"

"Wow," says Lindy. "Hawaii! I had no idea!"

"I can tell you this much," says Luba. "The purpose of this trip is clandestine, so the less you know the better. I'll handle fake paperwork for the dog, and put a harness on him. I'll pretend he's my emotional support service dog until we clear security. Sorry about the harness, Andy. It's just for show. And sorry I called you weird. But you are weird, for a dog."

"I'd like a window seat," says Andy, taking advantage of Luba's momentary sweetness.

"I see you in a Hawaiian shirt," Lindy says to the dog. "And a mini lei around your neck. I see you lying on the beach in sunglasses."

Andy pretends he doesn't hear her. It isn't the first time.

"I've still got the travel agent on the phone, Luba Vilnitsky," says Lindy. "Our seats are confirmed for Maui. Too bad the Newport airport doesn't do commuter service to Portland anymore."

"Don't you want to ask Miss Vilnitsky why the rush to Maui?" suggests the dog.

"That would be MIZ Vilnitsky," says Luba. "Sorry, sorry," she adds. "I'm just wound a bit tight right now."

Senor Zippy heaves himself up Luba's face and circles on the top of her head. He looks like a tremendous green tiara. He's sad his mistress is leaving. He wants her to know his heart might break in her absence.

"Oh, baby, baby," croons Luba. "I won't be gone long. I'll bring you back a present, my sweet baby. I promise, my darling, my Senor Zippy."

"Yeah, Luba Vilnitsky," says Lindy when she sees that Senor Zippy has balanced himself and Luba has regained her equilibrium. "Why this sudden dash to Maui?" Lindy's fingers are itching to light another cigarette.

"You will find out soon enough," says Luba. "On a need to know basis."

"Luba Vilnitsky, look at me," says Lindy. "You can always tell us everything."

"Especially in times of trouble," says Zoey. "We've certainly leaned on you often enough and you've always made time for us."

Lindy bursts into song. *"Sometimes in our lives, we all have pain, we all have sorrow. But if we are wise, we know that there's always tomorrow. Lean on me when you're not strong. And I'll be your friend, I'll help you carry on. For it won't be long 'til I'm gonna need somebody to lean on...."*

Luba sits on her bed, shaking her head no, but waiting for Lindy to finish the Bill Withers song.

"Okay. Okay. Here's the truth," says Luba. "In the *Wall Street Journal* this morning was the smallest mention about a solar investment deal going down in Maui this weekend. But I never got an invite. I should be there, sitting at the table, negotiating with the big guys. Why wasn't I notified? That's what I want to know."

"You talking about solar gangsters?" asks Zoey.

"More like solar sexist pigs," says Luba.

"You're a solar investor?" asks Lindy, giving in and lighting another extra long More Menthol. "How come we didn't know this? Just another of your secrets?"

"Sure," says Luba. "Just one more mystery about me." Then

she adds, "Oh for heaven's sake, Lindy, how could you not know? I've been investing in solar for decades. Just look at all the solar panels on Senor Zippy's habitat. And, Lindy, please, please, please don't smoke in my bedroom."

"Sorry, sorry, sorry," says Lindy. "I'm trying to quit." She places the cigarette with the barely scorched tip next to the stub in the white clamshell. She eyes them longingly.

"A Secret Service dog?" Zoey asks Andy again. "Is that really a thing?"

Again, Andy ignores the question. To Luba he says, "Senor Zippy wants a taste of apricot hamantaschen."

"Oh, my little Zippy," coos Luba. "You want a cookie? A sweet for my sweet? My good little boy."

"You're trying to change the subject," says Lindy. "Luba Vilnitsky, please tell us what's really going on or we can't help you."

"Okay. Okay," says Luba. "It's like this… First, I'll crash a weekend of meetings for the richest solar investors in the world and use the opportunity to do some sleuthing. I'll figure out who's really in charge of the operation, where their solar experimental station is located, what they're testing, and if I like what I see, I'll snatch a bunch of shares from under their conceited, privileged, white, arrogant male noses and amass enough power so they'll take me seriously."

"Ohhhh!" says Zoey. "That right there is the revenge part Andy was talking about."

"As for you two," continues Luba, "count on there being socialization. You know, a cocktail party, a bit of surveillance, some pool time, mingling with rich assholes, a bit of spying, maybe illegal entry. That kind of thing. Andy will need to hover near me,

The Jew Girls Adventure Series

but I'd like the two of you to cozy up to whoever looks out of place or too good to be true. Okay? Now you're in on the whole shebang. You'll both probably need gold lamé bathing suits."

"I plan to swim in my underwear," says Zoey.

"Don't worry, *bubbelah*," says Lindy to Zoey. "We'll pick up something appropriate for you in Hawaii."

"There's something else you should know," says Luba. "Elon Musk will be there."

"The self-driving Tesla guy?" asks Lindy. "The SpaceX founder who wants to create a colony on Mars?"

"You know him?" Zoey asks.

"I know he's on the list of invitees and I know the address of where they're meeting," says Luba. "A private home. With a landing strip. I know the man who owns that estate."

"You think Musk will start a canine population on Mars?" asks Andy.

"No," says Luba to Andy, then turns back to her friends. "Musk is huge in solar. He provides solar-powered energy systems in disaster areas. He built the largest solar panel production plant in the world in Buffalo, New York. Now he's thinking of doing something in Hawaii. That's why the big guys are flocking to Maui."

Lindy's fingers caress the green letters of the pack of More Menthols clutched in her left hand. Her right palm grips her lighter. Her thumb is ready to press the lever to release the flame. "And why is it you feel the need to join them?" she asks.

"Well," says Luba. "I had this really great idea for adding a silica shield to make solar panels anti-reflective, so I sent out letters but got no response. I suspected that was because I had a

You Can Call Me Andy

female name. So I sent out the letters again as if I were a man and received a bunch of replies. You have no idea how angry that made me. And then I found out experiments using anti-reflective shields are underway in Maui."

"You have to show up posing as a man?" Lindy asks Luba.

"No, no, no. That's not what I mean," says Luba. "I tracked a rumor that he-who-shall-not-be-named—you know, a certain big shot ex-politico now ensconced on a golf course in Florida—is sending a representative who will pretend to be an investor, but is actually tasked with instigating a forced takeover to shut down those experiments. I want to make sure that doesn't happen."

"Do we assume his best friends, the Russians, are financing the con?" asks Zoey. "Wait!" she adds. "Russian is too obvious. Wouldn't it be more like him to send a Russian pretending to be something else? French perhaps?"

"Interesting you say that, Zoey," says Luba. "Yes, French. But, Zoey, how would you know a detail like that?"

Zoey shrugs. "I didn't," she says. "The word just popped out of my mouth."

"I've been checking in on the Maui silica experiments because the developers seem to be testing a silica design similar to what I came up with," says Luba. "If they're calling in investors, it means production release time is near. And if that technology will be commercially available, I'd like to try it here in Newport."

"That's exactly what I've been fighting for all these years!" says Zoey.

"I know, *bubbelah*," says Luba. "I'm on your side. I think it should be done."

"And you didn't tell me about your plan?" asks Zoey. "I think my feelings are hurt."

The Jew Girls Adventure Series

"Look," says Luba. "It all came about suddenly. The notice of this weekend's meeting took me by surprise. I'd like to get myself appointed to the board of directors."

Zoey's logical mind is trying to make sense of the plot but there's still a lot of missing information. "Luba," she says, "what kind of revenge are you planning?"

"Well," Luba says. "I'm not sure how it will shake out. I should have been on the list of invitees and I just can't take the disrespect anymore. I've got to stand up and let those guys know they can't treat women this way."

"All right, but be careful," says Zoey. "Even if you succeed you might lose. That's how vengeance works."

"And now you'll both be there to protect me and keep me safe," says Luba smiling. "I'm glad you're coming with me."

"Us and the dog," says Zoey.

"Of course, the dog," says Luba.

"By the way," says Zoey. "How do you know the guy who owns the house where the soiree will take place?"

"What soiree?" asks Lindy, a slight petulance in her voice.

"She means the cocktail party that opens the weekend meetings," says Luba. "The owner is just a guy I used to know in my radical days. He looks like Tom Selleck. No, I take that back. He used to look like Tom Selleck did in *Magnum PI*. He's probably just a fat, old guy now with a big mustache. I haven't spoken to him since he abandoned me in Paris in nineteen-ninety-seven."

"Did you love him?" asks Lindy.

"Oy vey!" says Luba. "That's a complicated story." Luba's voice softens. "It began way back in college when I attended a symposium on photovoltaic cells and the keynote speaker…."

You Can Call Me Andy

For a moment, Luba drifts off into her old memories, then abruptly regains command. "To hell with that! If we're going to catch our flight to Maui, we have to leave right this minute. We can chitchat on the way."

Lindy says, "The poseur will be exposed!"

Zoey shouts, "Renewable solar energy will save the earth!"

Andy says, "Don't forget the hamantaschen."

Chapter 3: Last Call for Maui

The three Jew Girls and the dog, wearing his Secret Service vest, speed through the deluge of rain that follows them all the way from the coast to the Portland Airport, three hours away.

'Last call for seating' is booming over the loudspeakers as they rush to the gate. They are the last passengers to board the plane.

After they're settled in their seats and waiting for takeoff, Lindy asks an obvious question. "Luba Vilnitsky, where are we staying once we get to Maui?"

"I didn't get that far," says Luba. "My friends burst in and shattered my concentration. My solo plans have changed."

"Listen," says Lindy. "We'll need a place with nice amenities. I'm just saying. With a pool and a hot tub, of course. Right on the beach. Zoey, would you check out vacation rentals on Maui?"

Zoey takes out her phone. Her fingers tap faster than the eye can see. A minute later she exclaims, "Christ on a crutch! Twenty-four hundred dollars a night if we each have our own room and no dogs allowed anywhere! So, okay, I've got a better idea. I used

You Can Call Me Andy

to know this guy, Gregorio. A jetsetter kind of fellow. He knows people everywhere. Give me a minute. I'll send him a text and pull the old damsel in distress ruse. Tell him we need accommodations on Maui. Sumptuous, deluxe accommodations. With no canine restrictions."

An in-flight attendant comes by to take their drink orders. Tomato juice for Zoey, espresso with half-and-half for Lindy, a Drambuie for Luba, and a small bowl of room temperature bone broth for Andy. Lindy hands out three hamantaschen and takes one for herself.

Andy savors his, then licks the crumbs from his seat. Smiling, his head cocked at that certain angle, he patiently waits for another.

"Okay, you guys," says Zoey as the plane takes off and the flight attendant comes by to ask that she turn off her phone. "Gregorio has a friend with the perfect place. He said the friend keeps a key under a conch shell resting at the base of a passion fruit vine in a blue ceramic pot just to the left of the side door of his cottage. Gregorio says his friend invited us to stay there for as long as we want, and will instruct his driver, Mordecai, to pick us up at the airport and take us there. He said to help ourselves to everything we need. Including Mordecai." Zoey grins and her eyes twinkle as she repeats Gregorio's final two words, "Including Mordecai," which makes her laugh.

"Mordecai?" asks Luba. "The driver's name is Mordecai? Is that some kind of Purim joke?"

"Maybe," says Zoey. "It wouldn't be the first time Gregorio teased me just to mess with my mind. But maybe, like his namesake who saved all the Jews in ancient Persia, maybe Mordecai will help us obliterate Luba's nemesis, whoever it is. We could use a Mordecai."

"Hey...," says Lindy. "I just had a thought... why are hamantaschen named after Mordecai's arch enemy? Haman was the evil anti-Semite. Why not call the pastries Mordicaischen?"

"Because the gist of Purim is, we beat him, let's eat him!" says Luba, dazzling them with a big toothy grin.

Lindy rolls her eyes.

Zoey scrunches her face.

Andy circles in his window seat, lies down, and closes his eyes. There's nothing more for him to do until they land on Maui. And besides, the last of the hamantaschen have been consumed.

Chapter 4: Coffee Ready Yet?

It's just past noon the next day when the three Jew Girls and the dog finally emerge from their bedrooms and gather in the kitchen of the Maui cottage, which is actually an enormous villa. Zoey explores the kitchen cupboards and finds an espresso machine and coffee beans that she sets on the counter. Luba's search reveals an unopened bottle of Drambuie in the liquor cabinet.

As Lindy joins them, she's singing, "...*Oh oh, deep in my heart, I do believe, we shall overcome some day. We'll walk hand in hand. We'll walk hand in hand....*"

It's the chorus of the gospel-turned-protest song, "We Shall Overcome." The others pretend they hear nothing.

The view from the kitchen is of a massive living room with sliding glass doors that open onto a patio and swimming pool surrounded by a luscious garden. Seeing Zoey glancing longingly at the shimmering, enticing waters, Lindy says, "Oh, go on, Zoey. I'll make the coffee."

"Thanks, Lindy," says Zoey. "You're the best."

Zoey walks outside and immediately strips down to her red underwear and dives in. Sunlight sparkles off the quiet circles that form at her entry point. Andy joins her when she reaches the shallow end. They do a synchronized crawl.

As the coffee machine starts to poof steam, Lindy, still humming her tune, watches her friend and the dog swim laps, twenty-five strokes from shallow to deep end, back and forth, over and over. It's mesmerizing.

"Coffee soon, Bella Abzug?" asks Luba, interrupting Lindy's stupor.

"Soon," sighs Lindy as she lights a cigarette. She doesn't move. "Soon-ish," she says after a pause. "Don't rush me. I love it when you call me Bella. She was my favorite socialist, feminist, environmental activist."

"Abzug was a wolf in sheep's clothing. And you're a wolf in sheep's clothing," says Luba.

"Luba, stop. It's too early for provocation," says Lindy. Another long moment goes by before she adds softly, "Besides, *nudnik*, you're the wolf, Luba Vilnitsky."

Luba laughs. Of course Lindy is right. In silence, they both stare outside, stupidly hypnotized by the glare of the sun on the water and Zoey's and Andy's repetitive strokes.

As the scent of brewing coffee awakens their brain cells, Lindy asks, "You think the white stretch limo is a bit much for us?"

"Zoey's friend made the arrangements," Luba replies. "Are you asking, should we instruct our driver to trade it in for a sedan? The answer is no. A white limo with a good-looking chauffeur projects exactly the impression we need to make."

You Can Call Me Andy

Lindy checks her creamy pink nails. She'll need a manicure before tonight's gala. "What's the plan for today?" she asks.

"My plan is to take a shower," says Luba. "Then research the background of the investors likely to be at the cocktail party. I'll need Andy in case my search requires complicated algorithmic codes."

Lindy laughs. "I've never met a dog that loves writing computer code as much as he does. Wait a minute!" she adds. "I just made the connection. The party tonight is at the home of Tom Selleck?"

"No...I already said... he's not Tom Selleck. He just looks like Tom Selleck," says Luba. "He *used* to look like Tom Selleck. *Oy*, I'm starving. Is there any food in this house?"

Lindy stubs out the cigarette and obediently heads back to the kitchen.

"You really should give up nicotine," says Luba.

"Right, right, right. I'm trying," says Lindy. Then she calls out, "Eggs, yogurt, goat cheese, cheddar. Lox, bagels, champagne, and a bin of fresh vegetables and lots of fruit. I could make an egg stir-fry and cube up stuff for a fruit bowl. And if I can find a toaster, I'll slice the bagels."

"Are they gluten-free?" asks Luba.

"Probably not," replies Lindy.

"Any hamantaschen left?" asks Luba.

"We finished those on the plane," says Lindy.

"Is there any chocolate?" asks Luba.

Lindy checks the cupboards. "Lots of dark chocolate," she says.

The Jew Girls Adventure Series

Zoey enters wearing a bath towel, but leaves footprint puddles across the flagstone floor. She eyes the food on the counter. "You think Mordecai, our driver, brought in all this for us? Or does it belong to the owner?"

The three of them look at the enticing provisions and wonder.

"It's for us," Luba decides as she grabs the Drambuie bottle. "Because we're hungry and because it's here. Besides, didn't you say your friend said to help ourselves to anything?"

The others nod and Lindy begins chopping vegetables. Zoey starts breaking eggs.

"So, Luba Vilnitsky," says Zoey. "I hear you and Andy will be tied up here at the cottage this afternoon, but do you need Lindy and me to do anything? We're here to help. We want to help."

"Wait!" interjects Lindy before Luba can give them an assignment. "If we aren't absolutely needed, Zoey and I should shop for outfits appropriate for the rich-people's gathering tonight."

"Don't worry about that," says Luba. "I brought the fancy brown caftan for myself, but I can loan something similar to both of you."

"Oh, no," says Lindy. "No offense, Luba Vilnitsky, but everything you own is brown. We're in Hawaii for god's sake! We're supposed to fit in. Maybe we could ask Mordecai to take us to some high-end dress shop. I'll charge everything as a business expense."

"My clothes are not just brown," says Luba. "They are various shades of brown. There are thousands of browns. You know damn well I'm ahead of the fashion curve. Just you watch—next year, brown will be the new color."

Lindy and Zoey exchange a glance and purse their lips tight.

You Can Call Me Andy

"Okay, okay," says Luba. "But promise me, no tie-dye for Zoey. It's a formal cocktail party. You're posing as investors. Do whatever you need to look the part. And Lindy, since you're so talented in the art of seduction, tonight I'd like you to select a potential target then pour on the charm and get the guy to talk. Zoey, your job is to snoop and record, but be discreet. Leave no trace. Any last minute thoughts?"

"Please light up a doobie for me, Lindy," says Zoey. "No way I'm clothes shopping straight."

Chapter 5: Stylin' By The Surf

Lindy and Zoey both chose black, with contrasting accents.

Lindy selected silk slacks and a shear black top over a plum-colored camisole. Zoey chose a sleeveless raw silk sheath with a low neckline and a single diamond hanging from a sterling silver wire for her throat.

There had been a heated discussion at Esther's Shoe Salon about sandal selection, but Mordecai broke the impasse. Silver gladiators for Lindy, and black handmade Italian thong sandals for Zoey. Then Mordecai drove them to Vashti's Spa Maui for hair styling, pedicures, and an hour massage. Mordecai said he'd be leaving them there while he went off to fetch an outfit for the dog. He came back with a black silk bowtie with silver glitter highlights and four black glitter party spats.

Back at the cottage, Lindy asks Mordecai if he would prepare a pre-party cocktail to get them in the mood. When he returns, he's carrying a frosty Maui Ice Tea in each hand. Zoey asks him what's in the drink.

You Can Call Me Andy

Mordecai says, "Vodka, tequila, rum, gin, and triple sec, m'lady."

"Perfect!" says Lindy.

"Cool," says Zoey.

"Ladies, you must dress now," says Mordecai. "My instructions from Miss Luba are to depart for the cocktail party in twenty minutes."

"That's MIZ Luba Vilnitsky," shouts Zoey and Lindy simultaneously, mimicking their friend. Zoey rolls off the couch onto the floor. The drink is surprisingly strong and she can't stop laughing.

A half-hour later, Lindy, Zoey, and Andy stand in front of the floor-to-ceiling vestibule mirror and declare themselves ready. Luba, jazzed up in a heavily beaded brown caftan and a Tahitian pearl choker, hurries to join them. She scrutinizes her friends. "Okay. You'll do," she says. Then she smiles and adds, "You sure clean up nice, Andy."

Mordecai exits first, holding the door open for the three women and the dog. As they stoop to enter the limo, Mordecai offers each woman a helping hand. The dog waits patiently while they arrange themselves on the supple white leather seats, then he takes his place next to Zoey.

"By the way, did you notice the *mezuzah* attached to the frame of the front door?" Zoey asks in her quietest voice.

"Yes!" replies Lindy in a raspy whisper. They open their eyes big to indicate emphasis. "The owner must be Jewish!"

Mordecai's route takes them on a narrow, winding road past long stretches of beach and miles and miles of blooming hibiscus. The Jew Girls don't say much and Mordecai doesn't speak at all.

Finally, after they pass a large tract of undeveloped state land, Mordecai turns left and enters a driveway through an enormous wrought iron gateway. Half-hidden is a landing strip with five private jets lined up like bullets. The limo comes to a stop beside an expansive terrace encircled by palms and manicured gardens of scented flowering plants. A volcano is visible in the distance. Suited men talk in small groups, and a gaggle of very attractive young women in slinky, shiny, skimpy dresses mingle among them. Mordecai exits the car and opens the back door, extending his hand to help Lindy, then Luba, then Zoey emerge. Andy jumps out on his own.

"Here's my card," says Mordecai, handing it to Zoey. "Call or text when you're ready to be picked up. I'll be no more than five minutes away. Waiting to hear from you. No matter how late."

When he bows, then grins at them, Zoey has to stop herself from giving the dark-eyed charmer a kiss on the cheek in thanks.

The three women and the dog head towards the gathering, but Luba says, "Come, Andy!" then, "Excuse us, ladies," and abruptly veers off to the far edge of the backyard terrace where a handsome, mustachioed man is standing alone.

Andy, in his black glitter bowtie and spats, trots beside her. Zoey and Lindy watch as Luba and the man engage in an animated conversation—hands punctuating words they can't hear. Andy pretends not to eavesdrop but, of course, one ear is cocked at attention leaving his eyes to inspect the crowd. Andy is particularly adept at reading lips.

"That really does look like Tom Selleck," says Lindy. "Could he be the real thing?"

"Yikes," says Zoey. "Pure sex, if you ask me."

"Forget him, *bubbelah*," says Lindy after scanning the terrace.

You Can Call Me Andy

"Take a look at the tall man with the jet white hair and black shirt open at the collar. The one smoking a cigarette."

"Where?" asks Zoey.

"By the spa railing. He's talking to that round-faced nerdy guy and a big-haired handsome woman. He's the gentleman I'm going to target," says Lindy as she lights an ultra slim, ultra long More Menthol, exhales, and smiles.

"Good call, Lindy! Let's meander closer to check him out," says Zoey.

The scent of a Gauloise cigarette intensifies as they approach. They nonchalantly pretend interest in the view of the beach and setting sun. The man in question has a profound French accent. He's talking with a woman who's explaining the results of her 2020 Wellness Tour on the mainland.

"Is that Oprah?" whispers Zoey.

"Oh my god!" says Lindy. "It *is* Oprah."

"Where the hell are we?" whispers Zoey. "Are we even allowed to be here?"

"Maybe she's a solar investor," whispers Lindy.

"I want to touch her," whispers Zoey. "To make sure she's real."

"I want to make sure that Frenchman is real. Look how elegant he is," whispers Lindy. "Look at that tailored silk suit and those shiny black Italian shoes. No wedding ring. He's perfect for my assignment!" she says softly. "I'll take it from here. Alone. See you later, Zoey. Go touch someone else."

Zoey watches her friend approach the Frenchman. She dismisses the slight shiver that rolls up her back and prickles her neck. *Probably nothing*, she thinks, then circles the saltwater pool.

The Jew Girls Adventure Series

She nods as she passes a man standing solo. The man looks like Clint Eastwood's older brother. He calls out something in Hawaiian. Zoey nods and smiles at him, but keeps walking. She enters the house through folding glass doors that stand fully open to the outside.

From the other side of the pool, Andy doesn't turn his head, but his eyes follow Zoey's every move.

Zoey stops near the portal to assess the dining area, noticing the Chinese vases, paintings, ancient scimitars, and framed gold coins. She wanders into an office. Photos of the man who isn't Tom Selleck, with his arm around famous people, line the wall. She notes the three large computer screens on the desk, but just one keyboard. She presses the space bar, but nothing lights up. She opens the desk drawers quietly, finds a pearl-handled Colt 45, but doesn't touch it. In a left-side drawer she finds a folder labeled "Solar Investments—Maui." She flips through the documents but they're mostly numbers and charts. She whips out the cell phone tucked in her bra and takes several seconds to record it all. She replaces the folder in the desk drawer and continues in search of Mr. Non-Tom-Selleck's bedroom.

"May I help you, Miss?" a voice calls out.

It's the house manager.

"I'm looking for the bathroom," Zoey replies, forcing her heart to find a lower speed.

"You've taken a wrong turn," the woman says. "This is a private area. Please follow me."

By the time Zoey re-enters the terrace, Lindy, Luba, and Andy are nowhere in sight. She moves slowly among the small groups of guests, listening to bits of conversations, but the snippets make little sense to her....

You Can Call Me Andy

"…agrivoltaic potential to meet projected global electric energy demand."

"Energy can be converted, like compressed air," says the woman who looks like Oprah and speaks in her familiar voice.

"… blows through old gas wells under high pressure…."

"The lake of six hundred acres acts as a reservoir," says the man she passed earlier, who could actually be Clint Eastwood, now that she sees him up close.

Zoey feels the eyes of the men—and their statuesque women—on her as she walks down to the beach, but no one approaches and no one stops her. She passes a man with a gray goatee sitting on the arm of a deck chair who looks a lot like Kris Kristofferson. She hopes he'll pick up her mental plea to engage with her, but no such luck. So she keeps walking. When everyone is out of sight, she removes a joint and a lighter from her bra, removes her black sandals, and steps into the warm surf.

"Miss Zoey! May I join you?"

Zoey spins around. It's Mordecai. "Is that permitted?" asks Zoey.

"Permitted?" asks Mordecai. "I do believe it is, Miss Zoey, and if your presence is not mandatory at the solar gathering, it would be an honor for me to walk alongside you as the moon emerges. Your friends are busy. Miss Lindy with the French investor in the guesthouse, and Miz Vilnitsky discussing solar installations in the Baltic States with your host. The dog is assessing the property's perimeters and doing an inventory of the guests' vehicles. I hadn't realized that bowties could be fitted with transmitters that connect to high security databases. Quite a canine you've got there."

"Andy?" says Zoey. "He's just a mutt I picked up at the Newport Animal Shelter."

The Jew Girls Adventure Series

"Riiiight," says Mordecai, smiling all the way to his ears.

Mordecai is devilishly handsome. Zoey can't help but notice his assets. Full lips. Dark hair with a touch of gray at the temples. A nice baritone voice that vibrates some important place deep inside her. And he smells good. He's dressed in evening clothes, not at all like a house servant or chauffeur.

"Want a hit?" asks Zoey because she can't think of anything else to say.

"I'll be right back with a bottle of champagne," Mordecai says as he reaches for her hand and kisses it lightly. Then he removes the roach from her fingers and inhales twice, never taking his eyes from hers. He crushes the butt end between his thumb and middle finger. "Wouldn't want to start a fire," he says in his quiet, deep voice. "Please, Miss Zoey, wait for me here? There's a lagoon nearby I'd like to show you."

Zoey can't help but grin. She nods and the chauffeur heads back to the terrace. She watches his long legs take long strides to the area where the guests are assembled. The terrace is crowded compared to earlier. Luba stands out in her sparkling brown attire. She is surrounded by a small circle of men and seems to be arguing intently. Andy has returned from his perambulation and again sits alert at her side. Zoey watches the path until Mordecai comes back into view—a bottle and two glasses in one hand, a white fleece blanket draped over the other.

Chapter 6: Hangovers Don't Fib

Like the day before, it's afternoon before anyone stirs in the cottage. Luba woke spitting mad. When she enters the living room, she finds her friends passed out on the couches, and that just fans her flame.

"Damn it, you two *dumkops*," Luba calls out. "Where the hell have you been? And where's our limo and limo driver? I had to get a lift home and when I got here, I went to apologize for not spending any time with you at the party, but your beds were empty! I thought you had both been kidnapped. Or murdered. I had a terrible night tossing and worrying that I'd put you in danger."

Luba is dressed in a brown safari hat, brown camouflage suit jacket that emphasizes her buxomness, brown camouflage culottes, brown leather belt, and brown hiking boots. She also has a saffron and green Hermes Mountain Zebra scarf wound around her neck like a choker. The scarf is meant to honor Senor Zippy, the iguana, and to keep him close even though he is thousands of miles away.

The Jew Girls Adventure Series

Finally, Zoey responds. "I'm in pain. Is Andy with you?"

Based on the scrunch of her face, it is clear her canine isn't her primary concern.

"The dog is doing laps in the pool again," says Luba. "That's the wrong question."

Luba's shrill words wake Lindy. She opens her eyes and sees Luba's preposterous outfit. She smirks. "Ouch, Luba. Too loud," she says. "What IS the right question?"

Lindy reaches for her cigarettes and lights a More Menthol to trick the pain in her head into thinking it isn't there. Yesterday's bronze lipstick leaves hardly a trace on the filter.

"Luba *Vilnitsky*! My name is Luba Vilnitsky!" Luba spits. "And the question is, what happened to you both last night?"

"The truth?" asks Lindy.

"Damn it! Yes, the truth!" Luba shouts.

"Well, I met a terribly charming Frenchman," growls Lindy as she exhales a choked laugh. "Oooh, that hurt. Don't make me laugh. I'm in recovery."

"Which Frenchman?" asks Luba.

"Do you have any idea how loud your voice is, Luba Vilnitsky?" Lindy asks. "For god's sake, give me a chance to speak! The man told me he was scheduled to do a presentation today, or tomorrow, or sometime, about solar something. He smokes Gauloise. I was doing my job."

Lindy pauses her narration, but when she continues, her voice has a darker tone. "In the guesthouse."

Lindy closes her eyes tight and worry lines appear on her forehead. She shakes her head back and forth.

You Can Call Me Andy

Her friends glance at each other. They're concerned. Perplexed. They wait in silence.

When Lindy opens her eyes again, she says, "There was an absolutely lovely baby grand piano, just like I have at home. I just couldn't resist. Mostly I played Beethoven and Duke Ellington. *Oy! Oy! Oy!* My head hurts like a mother-trucker."

"How much did you drink, Lindy?" asks Luba.

"I can't remember," says Lindy.

"And you, Zoey?" asks Luba. "Were you with her?"

"I don't think so," says Zoey. "No, I'm pretty sure I wasn't cuz I don't remember any Beethoven. Oh, wait! I went swimming. I think I went swimming. Are my clothes wet?" Zoey looks down and touches her slinky black sheath. No, not even damp. "Wait!" she says. "I went swimming in an outdoorsy place. There was sand. And fish! A lagoon? Yes! Right. In a lagoon. Yikes! I think I went swimming in a lagoon with Mordecai, our driver. I didn't come back here last night? Then where did I sleep? Oh god, my head needs a sling."

"Lindy, could you *please* not smoke in the house?" says Luba. "I feel like I'm breathing the smoldering of your funeral pyre. Do you understand how irritated I am with the two of you right now? You had assignments last night. Your jobs, remember? You promised to help, remember? That's why you came with me. Does any of that ring a bell? You were supposed to ferret out crucial information from crucial players. But look at you both. You're like shadows of people who used to be my friends! I want to state for the record how disappointed I am in both of you!"

Lindy looks up in slow motion and enunciates carefully, deliberately. "Well, Miz High And Mighty Vilnitsky. I guess you're going to have to fix your own coffee this morning."

The Jew Girls Adventure Series

"It's past noon, Lindy," says Luba.

"Whatever," says Lindy as she shuffles into the kitchen. "*Oy gevalt*. Where the devil did I put that bloody coffeemaker?"

Zoey is lying face up, an arm covering her eyes. She looks like a reclining Venus in a painting by Rubens.

Andy is still in the pool, doing his laps. He snarfed down plenty of tidbits last night and now his tummy has an unusual swell. But no alcohol or skunkweed touched his lips, so he's the only one without a hangover.

Lindy calls out to Zoey, "Mordecai? Zoey, really? You hooked up with the chauffeur? That is so cliché! *Vos iz mit dir?*"

"What's wrong with *me*, you ask?" says Zoey. Then she sits up very, very slowly. "In fact, how dare you! All I can say is, that tall Frenchman, Lindy? Really?"

"The Frenchman?" asks Luba again with a shift in her voice, her curiosity piqued. "Tell me about him."

"Okay, let me think…," says Lindy. They all wait while she grinds the coffee beans. "Okay," she says again. "Obviously, I couldn't take notes, but this is what I remember. He said he was a fixer for energy investors. He said he was involved with financing at the international level. Something about exceptionally thin passivation layers from half a million oxy night rides. I have no idea what that means. Maybe the night rides are in a vehicle prone to getting flat tires and it's his job to fix them. That job probably doesn't pay very well. Oh god, I can't remember anything more. I drank too much and failed at my assignment. I'm so sorry, Luba. Luba Vilnitsky, I mean."

"But a French guy is at the top of my list of suspicious characters," says Luba. "If he's the right one, you routed him out from the get-go! Mother-of-God, Lindy, really. You might have made the perfect choice. You're the best. Can you remember anything else he said?"

Lindy lays her head down next to the coffee machine, deriving some relief from the sucking sound and puffs of steam. "I wish I were dead," she says.

"Lindy, listen to me carefully," says Luba. "Could the Frenchman have actually said 'hafnium oxynitride' instead of half a million oxy night rides?"

"Whatever," replies Lindy. "Near enough." The surface of the cool granite countertop is helping her forehead blood recede back into her veins.

"I think your French guy could be the thug I've been tracking," says Luba. "I suspect he's the imposter sent by that certain ex-politico holed up in Florida. And I think his job is to shut down Maui's solar experiments, or to take them over so they can destroy the technology. I overheard something about someone blackmailing Elon Musk. Didn't you notice the Frenchman talking with Musk when you first arrived? Musk was the guy chatting with Oprah. Did you catch any of their conversation?"

"That short guy was Elon Musk?" asks Lindy. "Wow. I would never have figured him to be one of the richest men on the planet. And, no, I didn't hear their conversation. He scooted away as soon as I approached," says Lindy. "I thought he was being considerate. I thought he was giving me a chance to flirt with the French guy."

"Coffee's ready," says Zoey when the steam puffing stops. But she doesn't move from the couch.

Lindy lifts her head and stands up. "Ouch," she says again.

"Step aside, Lindy," says Luba. "I'll pour it for you."

"Can I have some hair of the dog in it?" moans Zoey.

The Jew Girls Adventure Series

"If you need hair of the dog," says Luba, "check the surface of the pool." Luba chuckles. Her mood has improved dramatically since hearing Lindy's description. She adds cream to Zoey's mug, leaving the other two cups black.

"A shot of rum in my coffee will be fine," Zoey calls out.

"No way," says Luba. "Coffee only. We're on a mission and I need you both in tip-top form. Today we're off to locate a secret solar installation."

"A wicked Purim celebration would be more fun," says Lindy.

Zoey and Luba both groan at Lindy's attempt at a joke.

"I'm serious!" says Lindy. "We missed Purim entirely this year. Well, except for the gluten-free hamantaschen."

By then the hot coffee had crossed from their bloodstreams into their brains and pretty much won the battle against the pounding demons. Energy was reaching their leg muscles and increasing their heart rates. Zoey finally manages a standing position.

"We depart ASAP," says Andy the dog as he trots through the living room. He leaves a path of watery paw prints, but no one complains. "We'll be heading into rugged territory," he adds. Then he glances at Luba. "Dress appropriately, like Luba, but good luck on finding similar outfits. And, Zoey, bring a mega-gigabyte flash drive. Lindy, we might need lock picking, so bring your rake and pin-spinner. Be prepared for anything. We'll be taking the Jeep that's parked around back. We won't need our driver today. We should bring provisions."

As if on cue, as if he knew what was going to happen before the idea was born, Mordecai pops out of the kitchen with a one-handed cooler. "M'ladies," he says. "I took the liberty of preparing nourishment for your journey. I'll place this in the back of the Jeep."

You Can Call Me Andy

"Any chocolate?" asks Luba.

"Yes, Miz Vilnitsky," says Mordecai.

"Dark chocolate?" asks Luba.

"Of course, Miz Vilnitsky," says Mordecai as he bows and exits.

The Jew Girls look at each other, back and forth, and smile. Then, in unison, they lift their mugs of coffee, take a good slow slug, and close their eyes. As the warm liquid flows down their throats, their necks bend back, they breathe deep, and their lips part. No one else hears, or sees, their harmonized vocalization of "Ahhhhhhh."

Chapter 7: The Road To Hell Isn't Paved At All

It's taken a while, but Lindy, who's driving, is getting used to the clutch. She self-selected because one of the few things Andy can't do is drive a stick shift, and Zoey said she'd rather not. Luba is yakking on about what she's looking for.

"Some kind of industrial compound. Maybe a field that used to grow bananas converted into a field of solar panels. Probably not a garden," says Luba. "No overhead foliage. Full access to the sun. So, something visible. Could be a fortress because it used to be U.S. military property."

"You know, Luba, what I know about solar panel technology is nothing at all," says Zoey. "I don't think I'm going to be much help. I'm so sorry."

"Whatever," says Luba. "Don't worry about that. In fact, I need to take a moment to apologize for my snarky behavior the past few days. You two gals are the best friends anyone could ever have. Thanks for coming to Maui with me." Tears well in Luba's eyes and she says, "Oh, my dear *bubbelahs*, I love you both so much!"

You Can Call Me Andy

Lindy turns around, winks at Zoey, and says, "The love is mutual, Luba Vilnitsky. Here's to our friendship that perseveres through smoke and stupidity, alcohol and anger, miscommunication and omissions of fact. We all have our idiosyncrasies and I love you back for forgiving me mine." Then she lights a cigarette. She glances at the gravel road when the Jeep bounces through a series of potholes.

"I wish you wouldn't smoke in the Jeep," says Zoey.

"Well, the love didn't last long," teases Lindy as she stubs out the More Menthol and starts singing a Roy Orbison tune. *"Pretty woman, walking down the street. Pretty woman, the kind I like to meet...."*

Lindy has a good singing voice and although the others can hardly hold a tune, they sing along too. *"Guess I'll go on home, it's late. There'll be tomorrow night, but wait. What do I see? Is she walking back to me? Yeah, she's walking back to me. Oh, oh, pretty woman!"*

"So, Luba Vilnitsky," says Lindy basking in the applause from her friends. "Did you sock it to Not-Mister-Selleck last night? Mr. Non-Tom? Did the two of you hook up? Did the canary sing?"

Lindy downshifts like an expert into second gear due to the steep incline and serpentine curves.

"None of your business, Miss Nosy," replies Luba, but there's a smile in her voice. "Is there any liquid in that cooler back there? I'm parched. Not used to this Maui heat."

Zoey opens the cooler. "Here's the inventory," she says. "Grapefruit juice, sparkling water, blood oranges, Fair Trade dark Belgium chocolate with Pink Himalayan sea salt. Various flavors of yogurt. That Mordecai sure is thoughtful. Probiotics are so handy when visiting foreign lands."

The Jew Girls Adventure Series

"Pour me half a cup of grapefruit juice and fill the rest with sparkling water," says Luba. "Then pass me a chunk of chocolate."

"Was 'please' the last word of that sentence, Luba?" asks Zoey.

"Please," says Luba.

"I'll have the same thing that Luba ordered," says Lindy as she swerves to avoid a rather significant washout. "Please."

Zoey hands Luba and Lindy their beverages in stainless steel cups. Then chunks of chocolate. Then a wet wipe.

"Whatever sordid scene is in your mind about me and Non-Tom is fantasy," says Luba.

Andy stares at Zoey as if waiting for something.

"Sorry, Andy," says Zoey. "No chocolate for you. Dogs can't eat chocolate. Or have grapefruit juice. But Mordecai did pack a gallon jug of water."

"Then I'll have yogurt," he says.

Zoey nods and peels away the lid of an individual portion of plain yogurt. She holds it steady as he licks.

"Once upon a time there was more," continues Luba. "But now all we've got is a mutual interest in solar development. He let me down. I forgave him. He set me up and let me down again. That's when I was done."

"We're about to pass a dilapidated wooden gate, painted dark green," interrupts Andy. "Four hundred feet past the gate is a fork in the road. Take the left. Half a mile later, take another left."

Luba turns around to face Andy. "You overheard the directions?"

"Something like that," says Andy. "And, Lindy, you'll be tempted to take the first right. Don't do it."

You Can Call Me Andy

Lindy was happy to follow Andy's directions. That left her mind free to contemplate the aviator jumpsuit she found in the closet of the guest bedroom. The outfit she is now wearing. It's something like Amelia Earhart would wear, including the headgear and goggles. But Lindy is also wearing white Salvatore Ferragamo boots, and plenty of bangles and bracelets, which could cause trouble if she needs to trek through forest undergrowth. But definitely worth it for the look, she decides, and she could always refuse to trek.

On the other hand, Zoey is back in the faded blue stretch jeans she wore on the plane. Red and black waterproof Rockport high-tops with red laces. Her red underwear covered by a fairly new gray hoodie from Pick Of The Litter thrift store. Across the front it says, "Newport Cubs 2005," a remnant from a rare year the high school team wasn't league champion. And prescription shades. She applies Burt's Bees Ocean Sunrise Lip Gloss, just in case.

Andy is *au natural* except for the binoculars that hang around his neck. He deliberately left his Secret Service vest back at the cottage so as not to draw attention.

"Hey, I need to make something clear," says Zoey. "Just to get it out there… just so you don't misinterpret what I didn't say earlier. I think it's true that I went swimming in the lagoon with Mordecai. I wouldn't be surprised if I kissed him at some point. But absolutely, certainly nothing more. He's really nice. Intelligent, funny, gentle. I like how he looks at me, how he sees me. I find him quite enticing."

"When did you get…." says Lindy, fishtailing around a curve just beyond the wooden gate. The crunch of tires spewing gravel drowns out her final word. "Home," Lindy repeats.

"Home? You mean to Gregorio's friend's little cottage?" Zoey's laugh ripples off the windshield and bounces out the back where, of course, there is no window. The Jeep is open-air. "That place is a palace. I never want to leave this island."

Andy puts a paw on Zoey's thigh and sighs deeply.

"I don't know when I got home. I woke up on the couch," answers Zoey. "Oh, wow, birds! Look left!"

"Red-Tailed Tropicbird," says Luba without hesitation. "Frigatebird. Japanese White-Eye." She turns to Lindy and says, "Keep your eyes peeled. We're looking for flat spans. Wide open land."

"Then why have we been rising in elevation this whole time?" Lindy asks. "There are no flat, open areas. We're in a rainforest."

"I trust Andy's directions," says Luba.

"Andy," says Lindy. "Help me out. As navigator, feel free to chime in at any time."

"Continue on this road," says Andy. "Lindy, you're doing great."

"Oh, wow," says Zoey. "Did you guys see the Blue-Breasted Yellow Cockawallow?"

"She made that up," says Luba to Lindy.

"Polkadotted Green-Faced Kneejerk," Zoey continues. "Blue-Winged Yellow-Knuckled Boobie. Ooooh. Look at those cute little Brown Bitewings."

"Stop the car!" yells Luba.

Lindy stomps her foot on the brake and then remembers the clutch. The Jeep engine dies after a few minor lurches.

"Hand me the binoculars, Zoey," says Luba.

Andy lowers his head so Zoey can remove them from his neck and pass them forward.

You Can Call Me Andy

"Oh, yes! Oh, yes!" says Luba. "Look! A field of solar arrays. You were dead-on, Andy. Way down there, by the shoreline. See that? Geez, how do we get down there?"

"Continue on this road," says Andy. "This is the only way in."

"Red-haired, broad-chested, Hawaiian-shirted, blue-footed wayfarer!" Zoey calls out.

"What kind of bird is that?" asks Luba.

"It's not a bird," says Zoey. "Look where I'm pointing! It's a man on the other side of the road giving us the finger."

"Aloha, aunties," says the red-haired man who steps in front of the Jeep to make them stop. He's doing a shaka hand signal in greeting, but giving them a stink eye that no one interprets as a friendly welcome. "Who told you where to find us?" he asks.

"No one," says Luba. "We're just out for a drive."

"On private property," the man says.

"No, we're not," whispers Andy to Zoey.

"No, we're not," Zoey whispers to Luba in the front passenger seat.

Luba reflects the stink-eye right back at the man. "No we're not," she says. "This is public land."

"Roger that," says the man. "I be busted."

Luba exits the Jeep and walks over to the red-haired man. She places her feet in a wide stance and puts her hands on her hips. "We're just sightseeing," she says. "Bird watching. What's it to you?"

The man's threatening demeanor collapses, evaporates, and a nice-guy persona emerges. The Jew Girls radar remains alert, but the fur on the back of Andy's neck and spine relaxes and lies back down.

The Jew Girls Adventure Series

"All that brown camouflage," says the man after giving Luba a slow down and up examination. "I like it. Boots. Black cat-eye glasses. Real purdy, auntie. What brings three lovelies to wilderness on feast day of our Purim luau?" The red-haired man hasn't taken his eyes off Luba. "Don't usually get visitors," he adds. "Perhaps fate brought together, Miss...?"

"Did he say Purim?" Zoey whispers to Lindy.

"A Purim luau?" Luba asks the red-haired man.

"Ey!" the man exclaims. "That's right, auntie. Purim celebration. And you be dressed so fine!"

"For the record, my outfit was made by my personal tailor," responds Luba, tugging down on her jacket to straighten it over her slim hips. "I rather like it myself."

"What they call you?" Red Head asks straight out this time. "Looking at you makes me wanna howl!"

"What?" demands Luba. "Forget that! You said Purim luau. You're Jewish?"

"Of course," says Red Head. "Why else we be celebrating Purim? You be Jewish?"

"I am," answers Luba cautiously. "We are."

"Well! Hallelujah then, we all be Jewish!" says Red Head. "Us, me and my tribe, are second generation. Parents emigrated, mostly from New York City and California in nineteen-sixties. Ancestors kept the traditions, the stories, but adopted Hawaiian lifestyle. Our tribe domesticated this land over time and built a commune in the wilderness, growing our own Jewish babies. Could use more females, however. So, strange, foreign, beautiful aunties... you all be welcome and your timing be good. All-day fast is over. Reading of *Megillah* 'bout to begin. Drinking probably just getting started. Park Jeep here. Follow me."

You Can Call Me Andy

Luba pokes her head inside the Jeep. "Up for a bit of revelry, ladies?" she asks, then lowers her voice to a whisper. "We need to further strategize about what I cannot say out loud, but why not take a quick detour?" Luba's voice rises in volume again. "How could we pass up such a gracious invitation? It's your wish come true, Lindy. A wicked Purim luau!"

Lindy pushes the clutch in with her left foot, steps on the brake with her right, and turns the key in the ignition. The Jeep roars to a start. She puts the Jeep in reverse, then shifts into drive. As Red Head and Luba walk a path that leads to a clearing where a few vehicles are parked, Lindy, Zoey, and Andy follow in the Jeep, moving at a snail's pace. All three are hunched forward, eavesdropping.

"Brown outfit sets off sparkling figure," says Red Head to Luba.

"Back off, boy," says Luba.

"Just had a feeling," says Red Head. "I was on duty at high lookout and watched your Jeep drive up mountain for past two hours. Each time you had an option about which fork to take, you didn't hesitate. It was like you accepted my invitation to the Purim luau before I even made it. Like we both knew you'd come."

Red Head stops and turns around. "Your friend needs to leave the Jeep here. Our yurt village isn't far. My name is Oz. The name means Strength in Hebrew. People call me Ozzy."

The Jew Girls notice the improvement in Red Head's grammar. Was the jive talk just for show?

"Luba Vilnitsky is my name," says Luba. "That's one word."

Chapter 8: There Be Dancin' Tonight! A Purim Interlude

The scene is a raucous carnival. The celebration of Purim requires a feast after a day-long fast and the partaking of lots of alcohol. Purim re-enacts the Old Testament story that begins when King Ahasuerus of Persia commands his wife, Queen Vashti, to appear before his party guests so he can show off her beauty. When Queen Vashti refuses, she is executed and the King forces Esther, a beautiful Jewish girl, to become his new Queen. The story follows Mordecai (a brave Jew), Haman (an evil anti-Semite), and Queen Esther, who ends up saving all the Jews of Persia from total annihilation. This ancient victory continues to be celebrated every spring.

Traditionally, hamantaschen—pastries shaped like Haman's tri-cornered hat—are eaten, and the point of the festivities is to get so drunk you can't tell the difference between Mordecai and Haman. The holiday commemorates the Jews taking such a potentially horrible event and turning it into a celebration of strength, perseverance, and community. The high intoxication aspect never made sense to Lindy and Luba, but Zoey said the alcohol helps animate joy and they decided not to argue with her. You've got to pick your fights.

Here, in a forest clearing on Maui, the youngest children are dressed as hamantaschen pastries, with paper triangles covering their torsos. The Queen Esthers wear purple satin robes, gold sashes around their waists, and crowns. Gaggles of teenage belly dancers symbolize the defiant Queen Vashti. The Hamans wear black tri-cornered hats, costume beards that cascade down their chests, black tunics that reach their ankles, and rope belts. The Mordecais are similar to the Hamans, with the same beards, but their tunics are blue and white. The King is distinctive because of his gold crown, gold chest pendant, and gold tunic over a purple shift. Since it's Hawaii, almost everyone wears flip-flops on their feet. Those who don't are barefoot.

"Would you just look at this clan," says Lindy, spinning in a circle. Her bangles and bracelets jangle and chime as she twirls. "These are my people! I'm so happy, I think I'm gonna cry!"

A dozen small kids and twice that many teenagers hover in front of a simple stage. A robust woman in her late thirties, dressed as Queen Esther, is reading the *Megillah*—the story of Esther—to her audience. The youngest kids are twirling graggers—noisemakers—to show their contempt for the evil Haman. Their voices scream out Boo! and Hiss! and their feet strike the ground like thunder whenever Haman's name is mentioned.

An acoustic band is setting up. Bass guitar, two sax players, drums, ukulele, slide guitar, dobro, flute. The stage is crowded. A deep bluesy chord reverberates against the surrounding trees.

This is the wildest Purim party the three friends have ever attended.

Lindy is mesmerized by the hunky young costumed man on a bicycle powering the blender that's transforming fresh fruit, coconut milk, and ice into delicacies at a smoothie stand. A line of young girls dressed as queens wait their turn for a goblet of his fresh frothy drink. They giggle and twirl their hair as they watch the little kids go crazy in pretend fights between the Jews and Haman's soldiers.

Luba assesses the bigger picture: Yurts surround the clearing, but they're not just homes. Apparently, each one has a utilitarian purpose. Candle factory, treadle sewing station, basket weaving, pottery, day care, post office. There are fanciful rain-catcher chains on every yurt, and solar panels on the roofs of the yurts that receive full sun.

Ozzy spreads his arms wide in welcome, and the Jew Girls are hugged and kissed by numerous costumed people who circle around them. A young belly dancer, carrying a tray of drinks, stops and hands them each a shot glass of clear liquid.

"Even in the face of danger and fear," Ozzy says, "we should celebrate surviving another day. Lift a glass with us! Purim is a dark story marked by a crazy party."

"Okole maluna!" Ozzy calls out. "Bottoms up! Go Jews!"

"L'chaim!" says Lindy as she raises her glass in a toast to life.

"L'chaim!" echoes Zoey.

"Mazel tov!" says Luba.

The belly dancer waits as they down their drinks and return their empty glasses to her tray. She curtsies and moves on.

Andy spies a number of dogs wandering hither and yon in the clearing. He exchanges a look with Zoey, then slinks off to join the canines. Invisibility is an asset for an undercover agent.

"Let me introduce you to our big Kahuna," Ozzy says to Luba. "Adita knows these parts and is good at observing unusual

You Can Call Me Andy

activities. Just in case you need some suggestions 'bout bird watching. Maybe about the special sun-catcher bird," he adds with a wink.

Luba catches his wink and wonders, *Why would he make a connection like that? Is a special sun-catcher bird a solar panel? What does he know? Or suspect?*

Another girl in a belly-dancing Vashti outfit approaches with another tray of drinks. The Jew Girls know the drill. They each select a shot glass and toss back the liquid.

Adita, the big Kahuna, approaches and invites Luba to join her for a chat. Zoey and Lindy excuse themselves to mingle with the revelers.

"You and your friends aren't bird watchers," Adita says with no question implied. "There's only one other settlement on this road. Those men and their women come by helicopter now. The old military compound is still surrounded by armed guards patrolling the borders. We don't do anything to irritate them and they leave us alone. If you proceed you will be trespassing, so heed my warning to be careful."

"How many patrols and how often?" Luba asks.

"Twenty-four hours," says Adita. "Three men on duty at all times."

"Dogs?" asks Luba.

"No dogs. Too many mongoose," replies Adita.

"Guns?" asks Luba.

"They carry guns," says Adita, "but we don't hear gunshots. They're *kanaka* mercenaries. Locals. People of Hawaiian descent."

"Who owns the property now?" asks Luba.

The Jew Girls Adventure Series

"Some white guy bought it," says Adita. "The orgies have stopped. After construction in the field was completed, no one drives this road anymore. You're the exception."

"What's the land used for now?" asks Luba.

"I think you know the answer to that," says Adita. "And I don't need to know your motivation. You have our blessing."

Adita hugs Luba and holds her in a tight embrace until Luba's shoulders relax and she exhales a long sigh.

When Adita walks away, Luba heads to the music stage. Joints flow from sticky hands to sticky lips in the crush of pulsating bodies. There's Zoey, partnering with the drumbeat. Zoey would rather dance than drink or eat, but being high always helps.

Luba perches on a bench. *Too many mongoose?* she ponders.

A teen with another tray of liquid in shot glasses stops and hands one to her. *What the hell*, Luba decides, and tosses back the fiery liquid. The Vashti girl takes the empty glass and disappears into the crowd. Luba decides that was her final drink.

Luba watches Lindy step onto the stage and situate herself in front of an electronic keyboard. Lindy can play almost any kind of music and so she starts rockin' out with the band. She's laughing, flinging her hair in an arc around her head, and bouncing in her dusty Salvatore Ferragamo boots. A wild hour of ecstatic beats speeds by, but then the music starts to slow and the dancers form a circle.

When the band stops and the vocalists begin an *a cappella* Purim song by the Maccabeats, Lindy gives up and heads over to the buffet table. Meat at one end, then vegetables and grains, with desserts at the other end. Corned beef, huli huli chicken, cold tongue, poi, mahi mahi filets, ahi poke, borscht, kasha, kim chee,

You Can Call Me Andy

knishes, potato kugel, and, of course, hamantaschen, including a coconut-guava version.

Mother of God! Lindy thinks. *What a spread!* She lights a cigarette to keep from devouring the goodies.

Meanwhile, Luba has remained at the bench, refusing further drinks and homegrown cannabis joints as they sail by. She's enjoying the lingering peaceful cerebral float. However, her neat French braid has come undone and the top two buttons of her brown camouflage suit jacket are open. A man, dressed as a rabbi, stops in front of her, blocking her view.

"A penny for your thoughts, Luba Vilnitsky," says redheaded Ozzy.

"Oh, it's you," says Luba.

"You were hoping for someone else?" asks Ozzy.

"Just missing Senor Zippy," says Luba.

"Your boyfriend?" asks Ozzy.

"My iguana," says Luba.

"You are a fascinating woman, Luba Vilnitsky," says Ozzy. "Every word out of your mouth makes me crazy for you." He sits down beside her.

It's the Purim celebration's big finale and pyrotechnics light up the night. Ozzy takes Luba's hand, but she withdraws it. A moment later, she reconsiders and puts her hand back in his.

"What happened to your island twang?" Luba asks Ozzy.

"I can speak either tongue," says Ozzy. "Folksy when needed, but in real life, I'm a rabbinical scholar. I am also fluent in Hebrew. And Hawaiian."

"You're a real rabbi?" asks Luba.

The Jew Girls Adventure Series

"That I am," says Ozzy. "Also known as a spiritual advisor."

"Is that Zoey out there, fire dancing?"

"That she is," says Ozzy.

"Did Lindy go to bed already?"

"I think she's resting her eyes in the guest yurt," says Ozzy.

"Can you take me to her?" asks Luba.

"If that is what you want."

Ozzy's eyes close briefly and he emits a loud sigh made totally audible because the din of the revelers has died down and natural quiet has once again permeated the night.

Elsewhere on the property, the flames of a bonfire sink into embers and two dogs recline, haunches touching, both deep in their private thoughts. Andy had been engaged in a philosophical conversation with a sleek, sweet-faced, dark-eyed whippet.

When they were first sniffing rumps and getting to know each other, Andy explained how he happened to be passing by the commune and what the women he was with were hoping to accomplish. The whippet provided a detailed account of the chain link fence around the solar compound's perimeter and described where Andy could find the opening that would provide clandestine entry for the intruders.

Andy manages one final question. "You think consciousness survives death?"

There's no response. The whippet is already asleep.

Chapter 9: No Time To Shoot The Shit

The smell of coffee brings Zoey out of dreamland. She's on a futon six inches off the ground. Lindy is in the middle, Luba on the other side. Zoey gently touches Lindy's shoulder. Then whispers her name. Then shakes Lindy rather hard to rouse her.

"*Oy gevalt,*" moans Lindy. "Where am I? *Ech!* This bed is the most uncomfortable thing I have ever slept on. My back can't move. I'm a cripple. I told you I am not a camper! What are we doing here? Where are my cigarettes?"

Luba sits up and surveys her friends. It takes a moment to understand why they're all fully dressed except for their shoes, and in the same bed. "Where's my safari hat?" she asks.

"Where's Andy?" asks Zoey.

They look around the yurt. No safari hat. No dog.

The Jew Girls crick and creak and moan and groan until they're standing.

"*Oy vey*," says Lindy. "Again, such a headache!"

When they exit the yurt, the sunlight blinds them. Ozzy is waiting out there with Luba's brown safari hat in his right hand. He invites them to partake in the breakfast buffet.

Luba retrieves her hat but turns away from him. Ozzy's words make her head hurt. "We don't have time to shoot the shit this morning," she says to her friends. "Ladies, if you're hungry, grab a *nosh* from the buffet for the road. We need to get on with our day."

Luba turns and addresses the gathered clan: "Goodbye and *mahalo*. Thank you all for your gracious welcome. It was an honor to celebrate Purim with you. *Mazel tov* to all." Luba waves goodbye, then abruptly heads to the path that leads to the parking lot where they left the Jeep.

"Wait, Luba Vilnitsky!" Ozzy calls out. "I have a gift for you."

Luba waits. She actually likes surprise gifts. She doesn't get nearly enough.

Ozzy hands Luba a loaf of challah wrapped in a traditional felted bark Hawaiian Kapa cloth. "On this auspicious day after our Purim celebration," he says, "Jews are tasked with acts of charity. Please accept this braided sweet bread. The braid symbolizes the rope used to hang Haman. As you know, sometimes revenge can be sweet," he says with a wickedly friendly smile. "And nourishing. But revenge is not the same as justice. Be careful out there. Let me walk with you."

"I can't stop you from doing that," says Luba as she hands the challah to Zoey. Then she removes her saffron and green zebra-print scarf, folds it with care, and says to Ozzy, "This is all I have. Please accept this gift as thanks for all that revelry. I had a good time. I mean it."

You Can Call Me Andy

Lindy and Zoey follow close behind.

When the path meets the parking lot, they find the Jeep right where they left it.

"If you ever want to stop living in your big, fancy world, Luba Vilnitsky, know there's a place for you here. With me," says Ozzy.

Luba climbs into the passenger seat. "What could you possibly be thinking?" she asks him. "Look at you—a rabbi! Look at me—a decade older. Where's the compatibility? I don't have time for this crazy *mishegas*."

"But you are so mysterious and intriguing," says Ozzy. "I could love you, Luba Vilnitsky. I think I already do."

"Lindy!" calls out Luba. "Get this Jeep moving!"

Lindy places her left foot purposefully on the clutch, her right foot on the accelerator, and turns the ignition key. The tires spin gravel as the Jeep lurches forward.

"He's certainly a dashing man," says Lindy.

"Keep your eyes on the road," says Luba.

Lindy smiles and starts singing her favorite Jimmy LaFave song: *"There's a car outside. And there's a road. There's a time to stay, and a time to rock and roll. You've been a real good friend, but I'm on my way. If I don't see you real soon, I'll see you down the road someday...."*

"Don't you know any songs from this century?" asks Luba.

"Sure," says Lindy and she launches into Lady Gaga's "Bad Romance." *"Rah-rah-ah-ah-ah-ah! Roma-roma-mamaa! Ga-ga-ooh-la-la! Want your bad romance. You know that I want you. And you know that I need you. I want it bad, your bad romance. I want your love and I want your revenge. You and me could write a bad romance. Oh-oh-oh--oh-oh! I want your love and all your lover's revenge. You and me could write a bad romance...."*

Zoey and Luba chime in on the chorus: "*Oh-oh-oh-oh-oh-oh-oh-oh-oh-oh-oh-oh! Caught in a bad romance. Oh-oh-oh-oh-oh-oh-oh-oh-oh-oh-oh-oh! Caught in a bad romance....*"

"Better?" chortles Lindy.

Chapter 10: Break In!

"Stop, Lindy!" shouts Zoey. "I thought Andy would catch up with us by now. You've got to turn around."

"I can't turn around," says Lindy as the Jeep bounces on the uneven path. "The road's too narrow. Look for a wider spot."

All of a sudden, right after the Jeep skids around a sharp curve, there's the dog.

Lindy stomps the brake. And then the clutch.

Andy is sitting in the middle of the gravel road. The whippet is by his side. They're both panting hard, their tongues flopping as they breathe. The dogs stand, sniff each other's eyes, mouths, and butts in goodbye, and Andy leaps into the backseat of the Jeep. The whippet nods to him, then heads off into the rainforest undergrowth.

"There are no other turns," says Andy between breaths. "You're headed straight to your destination now. I was just down there, exploring the perimeter. It's a quiet morning. There's a hole in the security fence. I'll show you where."

The Jew Girls Adventure Series

Straight ahead turns out to be numerous hairpin curves, which would have been a problem if any vehicle had approached from the opposite direction.

"Look!" calls out Luba.

Lindy stops the Jeep again because she can't take her eyes off the road without driving over the edge. "So," she says after surveying the distant solar array, "how far is the hole in the fence, Andy? I think we should drive as close as we can get. I don't want to ruin these boots."

"We'll leave the Jeep here," says Luba. "This is close enough."

"Oh no, no, no," says Lindy. "It will be uphill all the way back."

But Luba has already stepped out of the Jeep.

"Tell you what," says Lindy. "I'll be the lookout and stay with the car. You can leave Andy here with me, for protection."

"Andy isn't here to protect you and besides, we'll need your skills," says Luba. "Plus, I don't want the guards to hear the Jeep's motor as we approach. We're all in this together, remember, Lindy? Didn't you make a promise to me?"

"Okay, okay," says Lindy. "But I say we drive until we can actually see the fence."

"Fair enough," says Luba as she climbs back into the passenger seat. "But keep your foot on the clutch so we can glide downhill without starting the Jeep and alarming anyone."

"But then I can't steer," says Lindy. "We could careen over the edge!"

"You'll just have to do your best," says Luba. "You're a great driver, Lindy. I trust you."

You Can Call Me Andy

Andy and Zoey in the back seat exchange a worried look.

Using just the brake, Lindy inches downhill at a snail's pace towards the secret solar experimental complex. She steers hard and is able to maneuver the Jeep into a spot under some foliage not too far from the compound's fenced boundary. The three women and the dog step out of the vehicle.

"Take us to the hole in the fence, Andy," says Luba.

"Wait," says Lindy. "What's the plan?"

"Wait," says Zoey as she sets a bowl on the ground for Andy and fills it with water.

"The plan is to enter the compound and then see what happens next," says Luba. "Hopefully, we'll find some kind of operations room. If the room is locked, Lindy, you can pick it. And Zoey can photograph whatever seems pertinent. If you get near a computer, Zoey, use the flash drive that Andy told you to bring. Download everything. We'll sort it out later. We need to discover who's in charge here, what they're doing on this property, get proof of investment fraud, and stop a hostile takeover. If that's what's going on. And I'll do whatever it takes to settle my own personal vendetta."

"Whatever it takes?" asks Lindy. "Luba Vilnitsky, this is just about solar panels."

"It's not just solar panels," says Luba. "Lindy, imagine it was you who was ignored, snubbed, disrespected, brushed aside, dismissed. Treated as if you were just a silly woman. What would you do?"

"Fight back," says Lindy.

"I rest my case," says Luba. "Let's go."

"Not quite yet," says Lindy. "You know me, Luba Vilnitsky. I

71

The Jew Girls Adventure Series

need to understand the why about something before I act. I'm trying to wrap my head around the connection between retaliation against sexist pigs and breaking into a solar panel compound."

Zoey takes the opportunity to do a few jumping jacks and then twists her body as her arms swing rapidly around to the right and to the left a few times. She rolls her neck in a circle, then rolls it in the opposite direction. She bends at the waist, letting her arms and head hang. She holds the position.

Lindy and Luba watch for a moment, shake their heads to dislodge the image, and continue their chat.

"Remember back in Newport when I told you about my discovery that silica shields could make solar panels anti-reflective and therefore a lot more energy efficient?" asks Luba.

"Yes," says Lindy. "Something about the technology being a game-changer for affordable workforce housing in Newport. That's the part that got my attention. But what I'm trying to understand is why it's necessary to break in. Especially if I, as the lock-picker, will be the one who goes to jail."

Luba steps close to Lindy and hugs her. "I'm pretty sure all of us will go to jail if we're caught, not just you," she says, a smile in her voice. "So here's the why, my good and trustworthy friend. At the cocktail party, I overheard two men talking about silica shield technology experiments on land here on Maui that used to be military property. So that lined up with my research. And they mentioned completing phase two trials. But the men swore each other to secrecy, so I knew I couldn't just walk up to them and ask questions."

"And that made you mad?" asks Lindy.

"No, that makes me excited," says Luba.

You Can Call Me Andy

Lindy and Luba watch Zoey doing a series of odd waist spins then bends to slap the backs of her legs. "Zoey! What the hell are you doing?" asks Luba.

"Qi Gong warm-ups," says Zoey. "I'm waking up my body to prepare for whatever perils we might encounter. I'm transforming into a mighty warrior!" She lowers herself so her hands and toes are on the ground, her arms and back straight, then she does a series of pushups.

Andy positions himself alongside Zoey and mimics her movements. They often work out together, but Andy prefers yoga mats to road gravel.

When Zoey stands up, she's grinning and her eyes have regained their sparkle.

Andy does a few extra downward dog stretches, then he too is ready for whatever adventure comes next. He sits obediently, waiting for the command to go.

Luba is more amused than she lets on. She turns back to Lindy. "What makes me angry is that con men are operating here and everyone is oblivious. I suspect your tall, white-haired Frenchman is in cahoots with that nefarious guy in Florida and they're working with the petrochemical industry to destroy the new solar technology before it gets to market. I have a personal stake in that silica technology and want to see it put to use. And, of course, I'm angry because I'm being ignored as a serious investor. The only way we're going to get to truth and justice is by breaking and entering. Okay?"

"Okay," says Lindy. "I get it. Driving to the front entrance of this compound, walking up the front steps, ringing the doorbell, and asking to speak to the person in charge wouldn't work in this case. The bad guys could be anywhere, posing as anybody."

The Jew Girls Adventure Series

It's impossible to tell if she's being sarcastic.

With that settled, Luba sets off toward the security fence.

Lindy speed-walks to catch up, her bangles clinking and clanking.

Zoey grabs the Kapa-wrapped challah loaf, tucks it under her camisole, and tucks the camisole into her jeans. She hurries after them.

Andy runs ahead to lead the trio to the hole in the fence that the whippet had shown him earlier that morning. He waits while the women crawl through one at a time.

Off to the right is the field of solar units arranged in straight rows like enormous Lego boxes. In the distance is an octagon-shaped building coated with some kind of reflective material. The coating makes the structure seem like a mirage... invisible, except for the door locks. The structure could be all windows, it's hard to tell. They crouch low as they move stealth-like in a duck walk to stay out of view. Luba remains up front, leading the way.

A weasel-like creature suddenly emerges from a burrow. Andy emits a high-pitched whimper and shoots off like a firecracker, running after the animal. The Jew Girls gasp, then cover their mouths. Zoey dares not call out Andy's name.

"Holy shit, what the hell was that thing?" whispers Lindy. "It's as long as the dog."

"Must be a mongoose," says Luba quietly. "Big Kahuna Adita warned me about them."

"What the hell is a mongoose?" whispers Lindy.

"Do they bite?" asks Zoey.

"They run," whispers Luba. "They're lightning fast."

You Can Call Me Andy

The Jew Girls remain crouched on their haunches pondering what to do.

The mongoose retreats into its burrow and Andy sticks his long nose down the hole, then his front paws so that only his rump and shaggy wagging tail are visible. Then he lets out a loud, painful yelp.

"Andy!" Zoey calls out in panic.

The others freeze. But it's too late. Suddenly, right there in front of Luba's eyes are two tan pant legs, both ending in a scuffed military boot. She looks up. The boots are on the feet of a security guard who orders the intruders to stand up.

"Put your hands in the air where I can see them," the guard says. He's wearing mirrored sunglasses, a flack vest, the whole military thing. "Walk," he says, and tilts his rifle in the direction he wants them to go.

Luba takes Lindy's hand. Lindy takes Zoey's hand.

"Single file!" he shouts.

"What do you think is going to happen to us?" Lindy whispers to Luba.

"No talking!" orders the guard.

The guard has them stop at an almost undetectable door that he opens by placing his security badge against a transparent sensor with a tiny glowing green dot. He ushers them inside, up a stairwell, and down a long corridor with a shiny marble floor. He stops them where a second guard is on duty. Although the corridor seems plush, everything about the guards seems cockeyed. Not quite sharp. Their mustaches are asymmetrical. Their uniforms aren't shipshape. Their rifles are rusty.

Guard #2 opens a door in the corridor and nods for them to

The Jew Girls Adventure Series

enter. The Jew Girls have no choice. They anticipated being held in a nasty prison cell, but this is more like a luxurious hotel room.

The men consult their ear buds and apparently receive further instructions because Guard #2 steps into the room and closes the door behind him. He stands at attention, his back to the door, his rifle at the ready. The guard speaks quietly into his shoulder, but his face remains blank.

In a very soft voice, Luba says to the others, "Come closer."

They huddle.

"What's the worst thing that could happen?" whispers Lindy.

"We'll be disappeared," says Luba.

"Not if we put up a fight," says Zoey.

"Let's just do what they say," whispers Lindy. "And be polite."

"No way," says Zoey quietly, but emphatically. "The first few minutes of any abduction sets the stage. If you go with the guy who says, 'Get in the car!' you give up ninety percent of your chance of getting away unharmed. You increase your danger if he drives you out to the middle of nowhere. We need to divert the guard's attention and escape this room. We need to help Luba succeed in her mission!"

Luba says, "Okay, my friends. We need to work on our story in case we get interrogated separately. Why we're here, what we're doing. The answer is we're going for a swim. We need to divert the guard's attention so one of us can carry out my plan."

"No talking!" shouts the oddly mustachioed guard.

"*Got in himmel!*" says Luba a little too loudly. "You and your white boots! Who hikes in white boots! Why did I let you talk me into this?"

You Can Call Me Andy

Lindy is a quick thinker and she gets where this distraction is going, so she argues back. She and Luba can holler with the best of them. East Coast versus West Coast style. But only they could explain the difference. "I didn't talk you into anything, Luba Vilnitsky!" shouts Lindy. "I should have stayed at the cottage. Look at my hands! My nail polish is chipped! I'd rather be sitting by the pool drinking a vodka soda than be imprisoned here, waiting to be executed. This is your fault, Luba! Don't blame Zoey and me."

As their fake fight escalates, they move in slow motion to the balcony.

Meanwhile, Zoey takes out the challah from under her red camisole. She does it leisurely, in full view of Guard #2. She makes a show of pulling off a chunk and munching on it. "Mmmm," she says facing the man. She positions herself to block his view of her friends when she offers the loaf to him, but he, of course, declines. Zoey shrugs and says to the guard, "Too bad. Your loss."

"No talking!" shouts Guard #2 again.

Zoey shrugs, turns around, and slowly walks to the tiny balcony, continuing to block the guard's view. Lindy is out there, standing alone, taking in the scenery. They don't speak. Zoey scans for her dog. No dog. No mongoose. No Luba either.

"Hey, Lindy," whispers Zoey. "You think there's a connection between this building being an octagon and Gregorio's friend's cottage being a pentagon? And why would militia be guarding a solar test site?"

"Because it's secret stuff," Lindy whispers back. "Hired mercenaries."

Abruptly, Lindy turns around and walks up to the guard. "Why are we here?" she demands, her head tilted directly up so she could look at his face.

"Are we supposed to offer you money?" asks Zoey as she approaches.

"I said no talking!" barks the guard. Then he snaps to attention, talks into his chest, receives some sort of response in his ear, and says to Lindy, "You! Come with me!" To Zoey, he commands, "And you! Stay here!"

Lindy is marched out into the corridor with a rifle aimed at her back. The door slams closed in Zoey's face. She's totally alone. Zoey looks around to see what's available to assist her should she choose to break out.

Farther down the corridor, the first guard waits at a closed door. When Lindy and Guard #2 reach him, he opens the door and forcefully pushes Lindy into the room, locking her inside.

"Expect a reprimand," the first guard says to Guard #2. "One woman escaped on your watch, and apparently you didn't notice."

Lindy can hear the man speaking outside her door and then the sound of his boots walking away. She paces the room. She chain-smokes her last two cigarettes. Then she gets really pissed. She bangs on the door. "Hello? Hey! Is anyone there? Open this door right now!" she calls out.

Guard #2 opens her door. "Stop shouting!" he yells back. "What is it with you women? Nothing but trouble. They already found the one that tried to get away."

"Luba?" says Lindy. "Where was she taken?"

"To the boss," he snarls.

"Who's the boss?" asks Lindy.

He shuts the door without answering.

"Let me out of here this minute!" Lindy screams. She pounds on the door a bunch of times. She gets no response.

Chapter 11: What The Hell Just Happened?

One flight down Luba's guard shoves his captive through a doorway and into the boss's quarters. Luba finds herself in an executive's office. A man is sitting in a swivel chair at an enormous desk. The back of the chair faces the room.

The guard steps out.

The chair spins around.

"You!" The Boss says, clearly startled. "You're the trespasser who broke into my compound?"

"You!" says Luba to her old friend, Non-Tom. "You're the boss of this military complex?"

"It's not a military complex anymore," says The Boss. "It's personal property. My personal property."

"You're the guy in charge of the militia patrolling this property?" asks Luba.

"Oh, those guys? They're not really militia," says The Boss. "They're leftover security. I kept them on the payroll when I bought this place because they needed a job."

"Do you hear yourself?" says Luba to Non-Tom. "When did you become a character known as 'The Boss'? What happened to the hippy eco-warrior peacenik I used to know?" asks Luba.

"You mean the man you used to *love*?" asks Non-Tom. "I'm just a businessman now."

"Imprisoning women is your business?" demands Luba.

"No, my dear, Luba," says Non-Tom. He smiles. "Solar investment and development is my honorable profession. Benefitting humankind and all that. Isn't that why you and your friends are here?"

"We were heading for a swim," fibs Luba.

"Where's your bathing suit?" asks Non-Tom.

"We don't need bathing suits on a private beach," says Luba.

"Your answer makes no sense," says Non-Tom. "So, okay, Luba. What is it you really want? Why are you here? I'd like the truth this time."

"You know what I want," Luba replies. "It seems you and I had a similar idea about silica shields, but you've got the prototypes up and running. Since I'm now in a position to invest in innovative solar design, I thought I'd check out your silica experiments. There's nothing complicated or secret about that."

"Well, Luba, I'm surprised," says Non-Tom.

"Why would that surprise you?" asks Luba.

"I'm not surprised at your interest, I'm surprised at your bad behavior," says Non-Tom.

"Excuse me? MY bad behavior?" says Luba. "You and I were lovers! I thought we were equals. You skipped out. No word for years. THAT'S bad behavior! And I know you've been following my posts online. I can feel you listening in when I'm interviewed on radio and TV. And then it turns out your Maui address is the location of a meeting of elite solar investors and you leave me off the guest list? And now it turns out you actually own the property where the experimental station is in full operation? Boy, oh, boy. That really ticks me off!"

"Actually, the bad behavior I was referring to was breaking and entering private property," says Non-Tom.

"We didn't actually break anything to get in," corrects Luba. "The fence already had a hole in it."

"Illegal entry is a crime punishable by fines and jail time," says Non-Tom. "It's one thing to trespass on land owned by someone you know, but you didn't know this land was mine. I could have you arrested."

"Arrested?" shouts Luba.

"Of course I won't," says Non-Tom. "But Luba, if there's nothing complicated about your interest, why not just pass me a note at the cocktail party? Give me a call afterwards? Ask me to set up a meeting for you with the guy in charge?"

"How do I know you're not lying to me right this minute?" asks Luba. "Is this even a legitimate operation? What's with all the secrecy around finding this place?"

"I love your enthusiasm, Luba," says Non-Tom. "Always have. And you're still a stunning woman."

"Oh, forget the phony flattery, you sexist betrayer!" says Luba.

"Luba, I swear I'm not lying. I am the guy in charge," says Non-Tom. "And it's all legit. You and Elon Musk," he adds. "Two peas in a pod."

The Jew Girls Adventure Series

"What the hell is that supposed to mean?" asks Luba.

"Didn't you have a chat with him at the cocktail party?" asks Non-Tom. "Didn't he tell you his goal was reducing the risk of human extinction by reducing global warming using solar energy? You two have everything in common."

"Creating cities on Mars is not my reality," says Luba. "I'm not interested in designing automobiles. Don't equate my interests with his. We overlap in just one tiny area."

"Are you blackmailing Musk?" asks Non-Tom.

"Are you out of your mind?" asks Luba.

"Someone is," says Non-Tom.

"Possibly the Frenchman," says Luba.

"What Frenchman?" asks Non-Tom.

"Tall guy, white hair, black shirt. At your house the other night," says Luba. "Smoking French cigarettes."

"I know who you mean," says Non-Tom. "That's the guy sent by the Florida syndicate. Odd that you bring him up. He flew in here early this morning. Without an appointment. Is that a coincidence?"

"What Florida syndicate?" asks Luba. "And what did the Frenchman want? I doubt his visit here was mere coincidence."

"He said he was looking for a foxy chick named Linda, or some name like that. He couldn't quite remember. He said the name started with an L," says Non-Tom. "A petite, brown-haired woman with lots of bracelets that he'd just spent the night with. He wanted to warn me about her. It never occurred to me it was you."

"Because it wasn't me. My hair is black, and I've never been petite, or haven't you noticed? What did you tell him?" asks Luba.

You Can Call Me Andy

"I said that no person named Linda, or any name similar to Linda, had been here," says Non-Tom. "I've had no visitors all week. But now you show up. Your name starts with an L. What would he be warning me about?"

"I didn't know about this place until now," says Luba. "And I've never even spoken to the Frenchman. And I certainly didn't spend the night with him."

"Well, the Frenchman said the L lady shared her plan to explore Maui to uncover a secret testing site," says Non-Tom. "He said he figured she was heading my way. Then you show up. What am I supposed to believe?"

"The woman he slept with is named Lindy," says Luba. "She's my dear friend, and she's here too. You've got her locked up! And our friend Zoey is in one of your prison cells too!"

"Those are guest suites, Luba," says Non-Tom. "Not prison cells."

"I was treated like a prisoner," says Luba. "Marched here at gunpoint. And, as you know, my name is Luba Vilnitsky. You can call me *Miz* Vilnitsky."

"My apologies, *Miz* Luba," says Non-Tom. "Had I known it was you, I would have commanded that you be brought to my private quarters immediately. And I would have offered Drambuie. You still partial to sweetened whiskey, *Miz* Luba?"

"I'm not here to socialize," says Luba. "What are you doing with all those solar panels out there?"

"They're prototypes," says Non-Tom.

"Prototypes of what?" asks Luba.

"Singlet fission solar cells," says Non-Tom. "This technology has immense opportunity for growth. It makes solar panels more

The Jew Girls Adventure Series

durable and more efficient at converting sunlight into electricity."

"Oh, really? How?" asks Luba. "Let me guess. You realized high-energy photons generate unwanted heat so you developed an anti-reflective and anti-soiling silica shield that doesn't need rain or water to rinse away dirt."

Non-Tom is once again surprised. Then he says, "Using silica, yes."

Luba smiles beatifically back at him. "Go on," she says. "Tell me all about it."

"Our research shows that solar efficiency drops as temperature and humidity go up," says Non-Tom. "And dead calm also makes efficiency go down, meaning some wind helps. We determined solar photovoltaic cells do best when it's cool, breezy, and dry. I figured we were on the cusp of a guaranteed moneymaker so it was time to invite investors, but I haven't filed the patents. It has to remain hush-hush for the time being."

"So, you're not a fraud, Mr. Big Boss?" asks Luba.

"I am not a fraud," says Non-Tom.

"Then why didn't you invite me to your investment presentation?" asks Luba.

"Because I didn't think it was the right fit for you," says Non-Tom.

"Because I'm a woman?" asks Luba.

"Because the minimum investment is a million dollars," says Non-Tom.

"But you didn't even ask me!" says Luba. "I'm prepared to invest that much. Especially if it is a certified B Corp. A Benefit Corporation. The kind that pledges social goals as well as business ones."

"I've already submitted the application for certification as a B Corp," says Non-Tom. "Give me the benefit of the doubt, Luba Vilnitsky. I haven't changed *that* much. I'm still a friendly altruist, just like you. Plus, I had no idea you had that kind of money."

"You have no idea what I'm capable of, in any arena," says Luba.

"Point taken," says Non-Tom with what could be a genuine smile.

"I want a seat at the table with the big boys," says Luba. "I want to be an equal partner."

"That's all? Go ahead, tell me what you really want, Luba Vilnitsky," says Non-Tom. "Don't be shy."

"Don't you dare make fun of me," says Luba. "Okay, there is more. I want a majority stake in the business."

"A majority stake would take twenty-five million dollars," says Non-Tom.

"Fine. I'll do it. I'll write you a check right now," bluffs Luba.

"You have your checkbook with you?" asks Non-Tom.

"I'll initiate a wire transfer and you'll have it tomorrow," says Luba, hoping her face isn't betraying the lie.

Non-Tom stands and puts out his right hand. "We have a deal, my friend," he says.

"That's it?" she asks. "You agree? No argument? No fanfare? And why would you assume we're still friends?"

"No need of fanfare," says Non-Tom. "Investment money is flowing in but nothing's been finalized. In the end, it will be my decision. I've always trusted you, Miz Vilnitsky."

"Okay, then," says Luba, standing up rod-straight. She shakes Non-Tom's hand. "I'll need a signed contract."

"Of course you do," says Non-Tom. He sits back down and speaks into his wireless ear bud. He speaks so softly Luba can't hear.

"And I also need witnesses," says Luba. "Get my friends down here right now. And the dog."

"What dog?" asks Non-Tom pretending innocence.

"Zoey's dog, Andy," says Luba. "Andy went down a mongoose burrow on your property. He might have been eaten. But you need to at least get his remains. For Zoey."

"Mongoose don't eat dogs. They don't eat meat," says Non-Tom.

"How do you know that for sure?" asks Luba.

"Because mongoose were brought here two hundred years ago to control the rat population. That endeavor was a failure because mongoose don't eat meat," says Non-Tom. "Plus, rats are nocturnal, and mongoose hunt during the day, so now Maui has a rat and a mongoose problem. Are you referring to the handsome dog in the glitter spats you brought to the cocktail party? Gorgeous fur on that one. If he is dead, can I have his coat?"

"What?" says Luba.

"Just kidding," says Non-Tom. "I remember when you enjoyed my humor." He speaks into his ear bud again. "There's a large dog, long hair, collie face, well-behaved, on the property. Find him. Bring him to me."

"Don't hurt him!" calls out Luba.

Non-Tom speaks into his ear bud once more. "Bring him back alive. If possible." Then he smiles at Luba again. "Twenty-five million, Luba Vilnitsky? Really?"

You Can Call Me Andy

Non-Tom's attention is diverted to his ear bud for a moment. "Your friends are on their way. You promise not to reveal any of the proprietary information I just shared with you until we go public?"

"I promise," says Luba.

"Look, Luba, it may appear as if I sold out because I've become rich beyond our dreams, but I never abandoned our principles. Losing you is the one regret of my life."

"You didn't lose me," says Luba. "You abandoned me in Paris."

At that moment, Lindy and Zoey enter the room. The disheveled security guards remain at the ready.

"I'm so mad I could spit!" shrieks Lindy. "Are you the boss? How dare you lock us up! We're just three ladies who got lost on the way to the beach. What gave you the impression we were dangerous terrorists? Who the hell do you think you are, you *draikop*, you *goniff!*"

Luba holds out her hand to stop her friend's shouting. "Lindy, he is not the imposter. Don't you remember him? He was the host of the cocktail party."

"Where's my dog?" Zoey demands.

"My men are out looking for him now," Non-Tom replies. "We don't get many visitors. Fewer still that come in through the dog hole in the fence."

"Oh," says Lindy. "I didn't recognize Non-Tom at first. Obviously, I was too *verklempt* from being imprisoned to notice the similarity."

"Non-Tom?" says Non-Tom. "That's adorable. I assume that's because I'm not Tom Selleck."

The Jew Girls Adventure Series

"This is his place," says Luba to her friends. "He's The Boss here. It's his solar field. His prototypes. He's the one pulling together the investors."

"Please don't call me The Boss," says Non-Tom. "The title is way too formal for an easygoing chap like me."

"Don't trust him!" shouts Lindy. "Don't listen to a thing he says. He's working with crooks out to destroy the company. If this is legitimate, why the armed guards? And why are the guards such messy *schlumps?*"

"Nothing is licensed yet, Lindy," says Luba. "It's all proprietary information. Secret."

"Don't worry about the guards," says Non-Tom. "They're just part of my jobs-retention policy. I provide excellent wages and benefits."

Andy, with a choke chain around his neck and limping on three legs, is dragged into the office. A second guard enters carrying a blue folder that he hands to Non-Tom.

"Andy!" Zoey calls out. She runs over, kneels down, and holds him tight. Then she inspects his paw, leg, and haunch for wounds and dislocations. She checks his nose for coolness. Her fingers find a thorn stuck in his cheek so she reaches into her bra and removes her Swiss Army knife. The kind with tweezers. She places the thorn on Non-Tom's desk. "What did you do to him?" she asks.

But Andy answers first. "Sprained my paw leaping out of the burrow. Heard you call. Watched the guard march you away. Waited for the throbbing to ebb. Heard the guards when they found Luba. Couldn't walk yet. Heard the guards whistle. Realized they would not shoot. Limped out. Went with them. I'm here now. All is okay."

You Can Call Me Andy

"What the...!" exclaims Non-Tom. "The dog speaks English?"

"That's proprietary information," says Luba.

"You can call me Andy," the dog says to Non-Tom.

Zoey looks around for incriminating evidence to photograph but other than the blue folder on the desk there's nothing of note. She puts a hand on Andy's shoulder.

They both remain on alert.

"People!" Luba calls out in an attempt to re-harness everyone's attention. "This isn't the fake investor. I've agreed to wire him twenty-five million dollars by tomorrow to become a major player in his business. You're here to witness the signing of the contract."

"You have twenty-five million dollars?" says Lindy, sotto voci.

Luba raises one eyebrow and quietly replies, "I'll explain later."

Non-Tom hands Luba the blue folder that contains their contract. "Luba, darling, you need to sign both copies on the very last page and initial all the other sheets at the bottom." He hands her a gold tipped fountain pen.

Luba initials, dates, signs, and places the sheets back in the folder. She hands the blue folder and pen back to Non-Tom, who ceremoniously removes the sheets, initials each one, and signs the final page.

"Time to celebrate," says Non-Tom. "I don't sign a twenty-five million dollar deal every day. I'll have a bottle of champagne brought in."

Lindy is about to agree, but Luba puts up her hand again. "We'll pass on the party," she says. "We have important business waiting for us at home."

The Jew Girls Adventure Series

"You don't have to go back out the hole in the fence," says Non-Tom. "Let one of my men drive you to your Jeep. Oh, Luba, don't look so surprised. I watched the three of you, and the dog, walk down the road and break in through the security fence. We have cameras everywhere. As soon as I saw the Jeep, I was expecting company, but I had no idea it was my good friend, Luba."

"My name is Miz Luba Vilnitsky!" says Luba. "And we're not good friends."

"Gosh," says Non-Tom, "And here I was thinking that since we're on the verge of entering a business partnership, we'd be on more intimate terms."

"Our intimacy happened long ago," says Luba. "A different lifetime. Why I was so foolish back then remains a mystery."

Non-Tom smiles at Luba. He takes a small step forward, his arms rising as if to hug her goodbye, but he stops and says, "Oh, hell. I'll take you to the Jeep myself. It's not every day I have the honor of transporting three foxy crusaders back to their chariot."

"Are we done here?" asks Luba.

Non-Tom shakes his head no, but he says, "Fine. Follow me."

In the Jeep on their way back to the cottage Zoey says, "You didn't warn him about the possible hostile takeover. Did you change your mind?"

"I did not change my mind," says Luba.

"Then what the hell just happened?" asks Lindy. "And where's this mysterious twenty-five million dollars coming from?"

Chapter 12: Filthy-Rich Dreams

When the trio and the dog arrive back at the cottage, Andy heads straight for the pool to cool off and to ease the pain in his paw. Zoey shucks her clothes down to her red lace underwear and dives in too. Lindy and Luba head off to their rooms for showers. They agree to meet in the living room. Soon.

Two hours later, Luba, dressed in fresh all-brown attire, was the first to arrive, so she lies down on the swooning couch. After perhaps a minute, she becomes impatient and calls out, "It's cocktail time! Can anyone hear me?"

Mordecai, the driver and apparently houseboy too, immediately approaches with a tray of three lemony drinks.

That's when Lindy, wearing an elegant outfit she found in her bedroom closet, returns to the living room and joins Luba. She sips the limoncino Mordecai hands her, then lights a cigarette.

"I'm in big doo-doo," Luba says. "I think I made the biggest mistake of my life. Where am I going to get twenty-five million by tomorrow? Lindy, I need your help."

The Jew Girls Adventure Series

"I suspected as much when you told Non-Tom you had all that money already," says Lindy. "And when you say you need my help, do you mean help coming up with millions of dollars?" She looks around for an ashtray.

"*Exactamente,*" slurs Luba. And they both laugh hard. The drinks packed a punch.

Andy pads in from the patio wearing sunglasses and smelling like wet dog.

"Oh, there you are, Andy," says Luba. "I have a sticky wicket conundrum. I need twenty-five million right away." She chuckles at the preposterous words she just uttered.

"Have you checked the bottom of your purse for loose change?" Andy teases.

"Funny," says Luba, but apparently not funny enough to make her smile again.

The driver/butler re-enters and removes the empty limoncino glass from Lindy's hand. In its place, he sets a small crystal dish. He looks at Lindy's cigarette then smiles at her. He bows and leaves the room noiselessly.

"I'm giving them up," she calls out after him.

"You could start right now," says Andy. "But we all have our vices and limitations. For instance, I never learned to cook, yet just like you, I get hungry almost every day. Is there a chance I'll be fed today?" he asks.

"Zoey will join us in a minute," says Lindy. "She'll feed you."

"I'll feed who?" asks Zoey, approaching from her slice of the pentagon.

"Me," says Andy. "Your canine companion."

You Can Call Me Andy

"Oh, right. Sorry about that," says Zoey. She's back to wearing the lovely black sheath from the cocktail party, but this time she's added a leather belt that's perched on her hips. She heads to the kitchen, sees Mordecai, and tries to ignore an involuntary quiver. She opens the refrigerator. "Andy, will raw beef, broccoli, and leftover brown rice work for you?"

"Sure," says Andy. "*Mahalo*. Much appreciated. My appetite is fierce today."

Knowing that the broccoli will take a few minutes to steam, and understanding that the discussion about millions doesn't involve him, the dog heads back outside to dry his coat in the sun.

"One moment, m'lady," Mordecai says to Zoey, using his lovely, smiling lips to form those delicious words. "Perhaps you would like to share limoncino-time with your friends before they pass out. They're both working on their second drinks. I intended one of those aperitifs for you."

To Zoey, it's as if Mordecai is speaking a language of enchantment. She can't comprehend the words, but she wants to do whatever he suggests. She takes the glass he offers and meanders to the living room, leaving Andy's dinner ingredients on the counter.

"I'll handle the dog's dinner, m'lady," Mordecai calls out as he watches Zoey sashay into the living room.

"Oh, Zoey! Good. You're back," says Lindy. "Luba needs our help. Wait! What was I saying? Well, I forget, but, Zoey, we were waiting for you."

"Am I late?" asks Zoey, still dazed by her encounter with Mordecai.

"No, no. We just need to enter the magical realm of money manifestation," Lindy says, and laughs at her own alliterative wit.

The Jew Girls Adventure Series

"That's your territory, Zoey."

"You need millions? Okay. That's easy enough," Zoey says to Luba. "Just stick out your arms with your palms facing out and your fingers facing up. Your hands will interrupt the flow of a narrow stream of money being transferred electronically through the ethers from point A to point B. Hold your hands out like that until whatever you need has coalesced at your feet. Swoop it up, voila!"

Luba is amused for a millisecond, but then sinks into a serious ponder. "I guess I could sell my antique porcelain ballet dancer collection," she says, a bit too loudly. "And Senor Zippy is probably worth at least a hundred thousand." Luba's voice cracks as the words drop from her lips.

"Oh, Luba!" croon Lindy and Zoey in unison. "Not the iguana!"

The three friends sit silently, their minds churning. They each mourn numerous dead ends as they careen through potential possibilities.

Suddenly, a flash appears in Luba's eyes. "Okay," she says sweetly. "Let's say twenty-five million coalesces around me and I exchange it for the titled position as head of a new socially responsible company that manufactures solar panels. Let's say I accept only green, eco-friendly people to sit on the board of directors. Let's say the company solves energy problems worldwide and wins hero awards for altruism and kindness." Luba pauses, and looks at her friends. "Want to become shareholders in my company and get filthy rich?" Her final words are a bit slurred.

"Sure," says Lindy as she finishes her drink and sets the glass down with a bit too much force.

You Can Call Me Andy

"Sure," says Zoey, absentmindedly sipping her limoncino.

All three drift off as they visualize their futures.

Eventually they realize Mordecai is sitting on a chair facing them.

"Welcome back, ladies. If I could have your attention for a minute?" says Mordecai. "I need to come clean. About two things. I didn't intend to ply you with cocktails. I kept bringing out one more to ensure Miss Zoey got hers. I take full responsibility for your inebriation. My sincere apologies, m'ladies."

There's something incongruous with Mordecai sitting with them in the living room. Then he says, "And I'm more than just your chauffeur."

"You're the houseboy too," says Lindy. "Oh, that's so rude. Sorry. I mean, houseman. Or is it butler? What would you like us to call you?"

"Actually, ladies, it's my house. I live in a private wing. And I apologize again for misleading you," says Mordecai. "Zoey, your friend Gregorio is a friend of mine."

It takes a while for comprehension to register, but Mordecai is patient. He nods at the dog when Andy walks in, a sun-starched scent emanating from his glistening fur.

"Have you told them yet?" asks Andy.

"I'm getting there," says Mordecai. "Your food is in the kitchen."

"*Mahalo* again," says Andy as he heads in that direction. "Thanks."

Mordecai's attention returns to the three women. "I also know your friend, the one you call Non-Tom. He is not the fraud, the liar, or the fake investor. Everything he said is true."

The Jew Girls Adventure Series

"How would you know that?" asks Luba.

"Because, Miz Vilnitsky, I was the angel investor in this enterprise," says Mordecai. "I provided the seed money and I've been involved ever since. Miz Vilnitsky, there are two things you need to know. First, if you really want the biggest seat at the table, you'll need a slight bit more than twenty-five million. Second, if you have liquid asset issues, allow me to assist so that you can complete the transaction. The assist will remain interest free, assuming you pay me back when the company goes public and starts making a profit."

Another long silence passes.

"What did he just say?" Luba asks Lindy.

"Is your name even Mordecai?" Lindy asks Mordecai.

"That's true too, Miz Lindy," he says. "My birth name is Mordecai. I was born the day Purim was celebrated that year."

His attention turns back to Luba. "Luba Vilnitsky, do you see this paper?" Mordecai removes a folded sheet from his pocket, opens it to full size, and holds it out in front of her.

It's an effort for Luba to focus.

"On this paper I've written my brokerage account details and my attorney's phone number. When you provide your account information, he will wire the amount in full. All you need to do, Miz Luba, is make the call."

No one moves. Comprehension is elusive.

"Actually, Miz Luba," says Mordecai. "Please try to focus. After you call my attorney, call your broker to have the funds transferred to Non-Tom."

Still, no one moves.

You Can Call Me Andy

"Can I make a suggestion?" asks Zoey. "That we go for a swim. I think we all need to be conscious for this conversation."

"But that would mess up my hair," says Lindy. "I don't want to get it wet."

"Oh, Lindy," says Zoey. "Just this one time, pretend you do."

With slow nods of agreement, the Jew Girls get vertical. They wobble a bit, preparing to walk. Andy gives them a wide berth.

"Ladies, I have some financial business in town. And a promissory note to draft," Mordecai says, bidding them adieu. "I'm taking the limo."

Chapter 13: Millions Of Oxy Night Rides

Mordecai returns to the cottage to find the ladies and the dog out by the pool. They're lounging like nymphs soaking up the bright Maui sun. By then, the alcohol haze has been whisked away by time and by the strong iced coffees Mordecai had cleverly left for them.

Mordecai hands each a soft, hooded, terry robe and says, "Please join me in the living room. Something dire concerning a certain faux French gentleman has come to my attention and we can't talk out here. And, Miz Vilnitsky, a package came for you. It was outside the front door. I placed it on the entry table."

Lindy reaches for her More Menthols, but tucks them away in the pocket of her robe. "I need to dress first," she says.

"Of course, m'ladies," says Mordecai. "And, Zoey, please bring the photos you took of the documents at the cocktail party. You may have uncovered pertinent information."

"What? Wait. What? How do you...? How would you...," stammers Zoey.

You Can Call Me Andy

"I know just about everything, m'lady," Mordecai says, and smiles.

The ladies exit to freshen up, but soon they re-gather in the living room. The dog joins them.

"So my hunch was right?" Luba asks Mordecai with no preamble. "There IS something fishy about the Frenchman?"

"I'm pretty sure the man speaking with a French accent is the fake solar investor," says Mordecai. "He could have been hired to represent someone else on the invitee list."

"Well, well," says Luba. "I think whoever is behind this is planning a takeover of the solar company."

"I agree, the fake French guy is just a hired hand," says Mordecai. "I was hoping one of you would have some incriminating documentation leading to whoever is calling his moves. Some actual proof."

"I've never met the man. But Lindy has," says Luba.

"Be cautious with what you say next," says Andy to Luba.

"Lindy, you'll need to see him again," says Luba.

"No," says Lindy defiantly. "The man was cruel."

"He hurt you?" asks Zoey.

"I don't want to talk about it," says Lindy. "I can't remember anything."

Andy sits down next to Lindy. He digs his nose under her hand and lifts it so it rests on his head. Lindy exhales, but her mouth is clamped closed.

Mordecai asks Lindy if she'd be willing to close her eyes and imagine herself back at the guesthouse where the cocktail party took place.

The Jew Girls Adventure Series

She nods and closes her eyes. After a moment, she recalls the Frenchman boasting about cameras hidden in a water bottle and a shirt button. The promise to intimidate someone with a foreign-sounding name. Something about a shadow organization. Something about dark money. And the half a million oxy night rides that she'd mentioned last time.

"That's hafnium oxynitride," says Luba. "Semiconductor compounds that effect water splitting. But, Lindy, none of that raised a red flag for you? You didn't think to mention this to any of us?"

"Well, the Frenchman warned me not to say anything, which shook me," says Lindy. "I was getting ready to tell you."

"Did he receive any phone calls during the time you were with him?" asks Mordecai.

"There was one," says Lindy. "His cell phone rang and he said he had to take the call but he stayed in bed. He started off bragging to the person at the other end of the line about waltzing in and having everything under control, but his tone changed during their conversation. He said, 'what woman?' and 'rejection,' and 'tender offer.' Then a string of curse words. I figured some lovers' spat. When the call ended, he smiled and said he'd kill me if I ever mentioned anything about what I'd just heard. Of course, I thought he was joking. Then he said, 'You have no idea who I am, do you, babycakes?' I thought that was odd," says Lindy. "I mean odd for a Frenchman to call me babycakes."

Andy leans his body against Lindy's leg. Oblivious of what she's doing, Lindy strokes the dog's head and her shoulders relax a notch.

"Thank you," says Zoey in an aside to her dog. "You're so good at providing comfort exactly when it's needed."

You Can Call Me Andy

"That's what us Andys do," says the dog, then he winks.

Their attention turns back to Mordecai.

"Can you recall anything else?" Mordecai asks in a soft voice.

Lindy concentrates.

"He said he was a fixer, and I asked what that meant," says Lindy. "He said he makes arrangements for people. That he's good at fixing problems. I asked if he meant things like plumbing, but he said, 'No. Not at all, sweetheart. I make problems disappear.' Then he asked me to be his bag lady and said I'd make an indecent amount of money, but that didn't sound like something I'd be interested in. I mean, what kind of clothes would I have to wear?"

"He asked you to be his courier," says Mordecai. "What did you say?"

"Well," says Lindy, "since I thought he was still kidding, I said, 'Sure, I'll do that, Mr. French Guy, as long as you provide me with an apartment on the Riviera.' All of a sudden, his mood changed. It was like he became someone else. He started interrogating me about the oddest things, using technical words I didn't know. He went from being a seductive flirt, appreciative I was there, to a real jerk, a *groisser potz*, a mad crazy insane *meshugener*! For no reason at all he yelled, 'Forget it! You know nothing! You're not who I thought you were!' He handed me my clothes and hustled me to the door. I told him I needed to shower first, but he wouldn't let me. I still thought he was pulling my leg, but suddenly there I was, half-naked on the outside of the guesthouse door. I felt dirty, ashamed."

"Oh, Lindy!" Zoey's voice soothes.

"Pond scum!" growls Luba. "Lindy, I wish you'd said something to us. What a horrible secret to hold."

The Jew Girls Adventure Series

"Just let me get a cigarette lit and I'll be ready to move on," says Lindy. She checks her pockets but realizes she left the pack in the bedroom on purpose. She considers excusing herself to go get them.

"Miss Lindy," Mordecai says. "I must apologize again. It is my duty to protect my guests. I am so sorry."

Lindy looks at their host with bewilderment. She sits up, back straight. "Thank you," she says, surprised by his chivalry.

"Listen," she says. "I need a minute. I'll be right back."

The others assume Lindy would return smoking a cigarette, but she's carrying a glass of water and the small package from the entry table. She hands it to Luba.

"It's from Ozzy, the rabbi," says Lindy.

Luba unwraps the gift. She holds up the object—a crudely hammered, small sterling silver Jewish star on a silver chain. "The note says he made it for me right after we left yesterday. I'm not sure I'll accept it," she says, setting the box aside.

Mordecai begins again, "Okay, m'ladies! Lindy, if you're ready to continue… In your role as undercover investigator…."

"Undercover?" interrupts Zoey, then blushes when she looks at Mordecai. She hadn't meant to say that word aloud.

"In your role as covert investigator," continues Mordecai, smiling, "you've tied together several loose ends."

"You had suspicions about him?" Luba says to Mordecai. "Why?"

"When I had my investigators go through the list of people who RSVPd and compared it with the original invite list, one name didn't match," says Mordecai. "We tracked it to a shell company of fossil fuel interests in Florida. We gained entry into their server and your name, Miz Vilnitsky, popped up. Apparently, someone there noticed your internet meanderings regarding the Maui meeting and decided to keep an eye on your movements. By following their keystrokes, we know they traced you to Maui through your plane reservation. But the three of you showed up and they didn't know which one to target."

"You'd think a bunch of rich white guys would have a better firewall on their Internet server," says Zoey. "It seems kind of delicious that three oblivious women unexpectedly muddled their plan."

"Not totally oblivious," says Lindy.

"I had no idea I was being watched," says Luba. "Oh, Lindy, I didn't mean to put you in danger."

"But it was me who targeted the Frenchman," says Lindy. "I approached him."

"Miss Lindy," says Mordecai, "you couldn't have made a better choice. The phone call you overheard appears to have been when the man posing as the French investor found out he was sleeping with the wrong woman."

"I don't know how you do it, Lindy," says Luba, "Once again, you gravitated to the right person at the right time in your role of fearless undercover detective."

"Thank you for saying that," says Lindy. "So, I'm not such a failure. Mordecai, what else do you know about the nasty French scoundrel?"

"Well," says Mordecai. "Apparently, he grew up in Brooklyn."

"The man smelled of decayed meat," interjects Andy.

The three women and Mordecai look at him. They realize he's been unusually quiet.

"And I suspect he's been to Non-Tom's because I caught the lingering scent of those French cigarettes in his hallway."

The three women and Mordecai continue staring at the dog.

"Don't look at me like that," says Andy. "You were all doing so well on your own. I didn't want to butt in."

"You might have mentioned your perceptions, Andy," says Zoey.

"I didn't have proof," says Andy. "I don't hypothesize."

"Your dog is a complex character," says Mordecai to Zoey. "He's correct. I received a call from the solar compound. The scoundrel planted a bug in the office yesterday morning just before you three arrived, so we know he heard everything discussed in that room."

"Non-Tom's office?" asks Luba.

"Right," replies Mordecai. "Non-Tom. I presume you call him that because he isn't Tom Selleck."

"Now I feel embarrassed," says Luba.

"No need, Miz Vilnitsky," says Mordecai, "the resemblance is remarkable. Non-Tom… can I call him Non-Tom too? Non-Tom said he came across the bug in a gold-tipped fountain pen the Frenchman left behind. A clever move. But this morning, on a hunch, Non-Tom took the pen apart and found the listening device, so he alerted me. He was concerned that you three women might be targets. Your power move yesterday will certainly draw out the guy. He must know he botched up big-time and stands to lose whatever his employer promised to pay him. More important, his reputation will take a nosedive. You can't make a mistake like he just did and still be a valuable fixer for the underworld."

You Can Call Me Andy

"This all sounds like the plot of a bad crime novel," says Zoey.

"Which reminds me," says Mordecai. "Miss Zoey, may I see the investor accounts you photographed at the house where the party took place? They should shed more light on this story."

Zoey hands him her phone.

"Perfect," says Mordecai as he scrolls through the tables and charts. "These documents track stock ownership and trades since the beginning. I should be able to isolate the Florida shell company's dealings and make sure no additional stock gets purchased by them. Miss Zoey, I'm forwarding these files to my account and removing them from your phone. And removing the backups. And erasing the path. For your protection."

"Okay," says Zoey.

"Are you saying the shell company was purchasing stock in small quantities under various names?" asks Luba.

"You already knew that, Miz Vilnitsky," says Mordecai. "Isn't that what roused your suspicions in the first place? All those purchases issued from Florida."

"You mean my wild guess about Florida were spot on?" asks Lindy.

Zoey gives Lindy a high-five hand-jive that ends with a fist bump.

"I sure could use a cigarette about now," says Lindy. Then she gives a sideways smile to her friends. "Maybe this wasn't the best time to quit smoking."

"You gave up smoking?" asks Zoey.

"That's great news, Lindy," says Luba. "I mean it. But I need you both to concentrate. Please stay on track. Mordecai," she continues, "you're saying nothing I do on the Internet can be hidden anymore. Every keystroke, even those made for the good of the order, can be tracked by anyone, anytime."

"I'm not suggesting you curtail your explorations, Miz Vilnitsky," says Mordecai, "but be careful where you click, and hyper-aware that your meanderings are visible."

"I can insert an extra layer of privacy code to improve your chances of remaining undetected," says Andy, "but not even I could guarantee your searches are untraceable."

"So, Mr. Mordecai, Mister Limo Driver, Mister Amazing Whoever You Are," says Lindy, "what are we supposed to do now?"

"I expect we'll be hearing from the scoundrel since he has unfinished business with Miz Vilnitsky," Mordecai replies. "But for the safety of all three of you, and of course the dog, I think you should leave Maui as soon as possible even though I'll be sad to see you go. You've been highly entertaining guests."

"It's too late for that," says Andy. "The future is about to break in through the patio door."

Andy's fur bristles and a low growl emanates from deep in his chest. His eyes are riveted on the patio door. A moment later, the tall, white-haired, faux Frenchman, carrying a sleek attaché case, steps inside without knocking.

Chapter 14: The Liar's Downfall

"Which one of you did I meet the other night?" the faux Frenchman asks in his faux French accent, a smirk on his face.

The Jew Girls glance at each other, their eyebrows raised in shock. Mordecai takes a step forward, but the tall man sticks his hand out and orders Mordecai to halt.

"You there," the trespasser says. "Houseboy, get me some of that coffee I smell."

Mordecai nods at Andy.

Andy gets the message.

"Okay, then," the bad guy says. "I'm looking for a broad and it's not the vamp with the daggers for fingernails," he says, pointing to Lindy. He smiles at the other two women, but there's no warmth in his eyes.

The Jew Girls say nothing, still stunned to find the nasty intruder in their living room.

The Jew Girls Adventure Series

"As for you," the man says to Lindy, taking a few steps closer to her. "I had a real fine time with you the other night. Remind me of your name."

"Lindy," says Lindy.

"Right. Lindy," he says as if he doesn't care. "I need to talk to you first." He takes another step closer, just inches from her face.

Lindy doesn't back up. "I remember you too," she says. "You're the liar with the faux French accent and fancy clothes."

"I realized too late that you have no proclivity for investments," the liar says, his accent beginning to slip. "But we left a few loose ends. I have a proposition for you. We should speak privately. Like outside."

"I'm not going outside with you," she replies, repulsed by the man's proximity.

Luba and Zoey step between them, forcing the man to back up.

"She's no help," he says without any hint of a French lilt. "So, we're on to the next piece of business. Which one of you is the real solar investor?"

The faux Frenchman looks Luba and Zoey up and down a couple of times. His eyes linger on Luba's bosom, then go to her face. "You!" he says, pointing to her. "You must be the real solar investor. Which means you made a big mistake, Missy. You just got yourself a twenty-five million dollar headache. I'm sure you couldn't raise that kind of money overnight, and playing with the big boys is going to hurt you plenty. But I'll tell you what. I'm here representing the board of directors. We see the predicament you're in and agree to be lenient. We'll allow you to withdraw your offer and tear up your contract. No penalty. You'll get something for your pain and suffering."

You Can Call Me Andy

"What kind of something?" Luba asks.

"You'll get a most generous kill fee of ten thousand dollars," says the faux Frenchman. "No strings attached. You can go off and do good somewhere else."

"Ten thousand is not nearly enough," says Luba, deliberately goading him.

"Okay, okay," says the liar. "Twenty thousand. And we'll throw in a hundred shares of the company to sweeten the deal."

Mordecai comes in wearing an apron as a disguise and carrying a tray with a carafe of room-temperature coffee. Sugar and cream are in tiny pitchers. He sets the tray on the table, pours a cup for each of the ladies, and hands them out individually, with a napkin. Under Zoey's napkin is her cell phone. She catches Mordecai's eye, which goes to her phone and back to her. She sees that a 911 call to the Maui Police has been activated.

"Nothing you said is true," says Luba. "And my answer is no. I think I'll let the contract stand."

"You don't want to do that," the man from Brooklyn threatens.

Luba doesn't respond, so the man continues in a kinder voice. "Lady, you don't understand, I'm doing you a favor. You're probably the type that likes watching a man beg. Okay, I'm begging."

"What happens if I say yes?" asks Luba.

"You get twenty thousand dollars and one hundred shares of a solar development company. There is no downside," he says.

"What if I say no?" asks Luba.

"You'll be forever in debt," he says. "But maybe that won't matter. Dead people don't need stock dividends."

The Jew Girls Adventure Series

"You're threatening to kill me?" asks Luba, her voice reaching the alto range. "There are witnesses here!"

"Then perhaps all of you will vanish," the man says. "I'm good at what I do. I finish what I start. I don't like loose ends."

"We're not afraid of you, Mr. Bad Guy," says Lindy. "Go ahead, terrorize all you want. You've got a lot more to lose than any of us!"

"Hey, hey, hey," the bad guy says. "Hold on. What's gotten you so riled, babycakes? You and me could have had something special. Treat me right and we still could." The man's faux French accent is completely gone. Now he sounds like any other thug.

"Hey, hey, hey, yourself," says Lindy. "You're disgusting!"

"And apparently, you're a fool," the man spits back at her.

"You're the fool!" intercedes Zoey. "You think you can get away with pretending to be a solar investor? You think we don't know you were hired by the Florida syndicate? We know why you're here, and we know about the blackmail! Consider yourself busted!"

"All lies," the liar replies. "You're all crazy. It wasn't me. None of that."

Mordecai leans down to whisper in Zoey's ear. "I didn't know about the blackmail," he says.

Zoey shrugs, smiles at Mordecai, and whispers back, "I made that up in case he's the one blackmailing Elon Musk."

"Ah," says Mordecai and stands back up.

"Heavy duty malfeasance!" says Andy.

The words come out as a deep-throated growl, which gets the intruder's attention, and for the first time the man notices there's a

You Can Call Me Andy

dog in the room, and that the dog's teeth are just a few inches from his leg.

"Get this dog away from me!" yells the bad man.

Andy lowers the volume of his growl but, of course, no one suggests he move.

"Do you have orders to instigate a hostile takeover of the solar company if the majority of the board won't go along with a buyout?" asks Luba.

"Absolutely not," says the liar. "My intentions are pure."

"Then why do we have proof that your employers falsified board member identities?" asks Zoey.

"Petty violations. Nothing will stick," the liar responds.

"Investment fraud is a felony," says Luba.

"Some operations require a bit of falsification for privacy reasons," says the faux Frenchman. "It's just business."

"You're admitting you and your employers committed fraud?" asks Lindy.

"Don't put words in my mouth, babycakes," he says to Lindy, then focuses his squinty eyes on Luba. "Withdraw your offer now, you pushy broad. I have the prepared document right here."

The liar uses a gold key to unlock the attaché case. He removes a single sheet of paper and a gold-tipped fountain pen surprisingly similar to the bugged one used to sign the contract at Non-Tom's compound. The liar holds the two items up to Luba.

"Or what?" asks Luba. She stands in front of him, her chin up high, her hands on her hips, her feet spread in a power stance.

"My friends aren't as patient as I am," says the liar. "They will be here in a minute. If I were you, I'd choose my next step wisely."

Andy moves closer to the man. His lips are tucked back and under so that his big, white canine fangs predominate.

They hear two vehicles approach the house and car doors slam.

"There! You see! My friends arrived right on time," says the liar. "Say yes right now and I'll have them back off."

"Why assume they're your friends?" asks Lindy.

"Because I gave them this address," says the scoundrel, but he pauses for a moment to think. "Why? Are you expecting company?"

"Well, yes we are," says Zoey. "I've been recording our conversation, and the phone line to the Maui police has been open since you walked in. I believe they've come to arrest you." She holds up her phone as proof.

"You're bluffing!" says the liar. "That's my ride."

"Here's the deal," says Luba. "I'm about to become the majority stockholder in the solar company, and you'd better believe I'm taking the prototypes to full market production. And the shares your fake buddies hold? Well, now they're all mine. You might be a despicable man, but I really need to thank you. You just made me a very rich pushy broad."

Luba made up the part about the transfer of fraudulent investments. In truth, they'd be put back on the open market. But just saying those words gives her a taste of sweet revenge. She's actually beaming.

"You're going to prison," says Lindy. "Have fun fixing that, babycakes!"

By that time, four police officers had entered—two through the front door, and two from the patio. All have their guns drawn.

You Can Call Me Andy

As they arrest the faux Frenchman, he tries to wrestle out of their grip, but they get him down on the floor and then in handcuffs, read him his rights, and lead him out. No shots were fired. Two officers stay behind to take statements. Mordecai, still wearing his apron, offers them cups of cold coffee, which they accept.

Once the police are gone, the Jew Girls shriek, leap, give each other high-fives, and start dancing like crazy Jewish banshees.

Chapter 15: Words Like That

"Where's Mordecai?" asks Luba when she stops to catch her breath from all that wild bopping.

"On the patio, chatting with Andy," says Zoey. She clutches her chest as if to cradle her heart.

Lindy heads for the mirror to check her hair and lipstick.

Luba taps on the sliding door and motions for Mordecai to come in. He does. Andy follows.

"I need a reality check, Mordecai," says Luba. "Please, have a seat." She sits down too. "Explain again your short-term liquidity assist offer. It's a staggering amount of money. I can't possibly accept."

"The money isn't a problem," says Mordecai. "I have plenty and I'm always looking for opportunities to support a good cause. It's my way of having fun."

Mordecai removes the folded paper again, and this time he hands it to Luba. "Make the two calls, Miz Vilnitsky. The first to

You Can Call Me Andy

my attorney to transfer the funds to your account. The second to your brokerage initiating the transfer to the solar corporation. With that act, Luba, you will not only have a major stake in the business, but you also become president of the board of directors."

"That's a guarantee?" asks Luba, ignoring his omission of Miz and her last name.

"Yes, Miz Luba," says Mordecai.

"Even though we both know there is no guarantee ever, for anything?" says Luba.

"Yes, Miz Luba Vilnitsky," says Mordecai.

"Are you and angel or something?" asks Lindy, all tidied up.

"I witnessed the swiftness with which you three brought a poseur and a cabal of criminals to our attention," says Mordecai. "The Florida syndicate had infiltrated our pool of investors and were about to secure a majority vote on the board of directors. We had no idea. We've been paying attention to the technology, not tracking the money. I'd like to continue working with you, Miz Vilnitsky. And your friends."

Mordecai casts a glance at Lindy, but his eyes settle longer on Zoey. "They're loyal, they're clever, and," he pauses a moment, "this one has amazing things tucked in her bra."

Zoey's eyes widen in panic but they don't leave Mordecai's face. Lindy and Luba look at one another. They raise their eyebrows. They fail at stifling their laughter. They guffaw.

"Zoey, can I borrow your phone?" chuckles Luba.

Zoey removes the phone from her bra but doesn't break her eye-lock with Mordecai as she hands it over.

Luba checks the paper in her hand and dials Mordecai's lawyer.

The Jew Girls Adventure Series

"Don't make fun of me," says Zoey. "This fancy black party dress I've been living in for days doesn't have pockets. And you know my motto is Be Prepared."

"We're not making fun of you," says Lindy. "We're admiring your ability to improvise. And my motto is Go Wild On Accessories," says Lindy, shaking her bracelet baubles. "They remind me to take time for joy. We should all make time for joy."

"Transforming the derelict ten-acre fairgrounds property into a pedestrian-friendly solar-powered neighborhood would be my kind of joy," says Zoey.

Luba provides her brokerage account information to someone at the other end of the line.

"Stay Hungry," says Andy. "That's my motto. But eating is my joy."

"It's Always A Mistake Not To Go," says Mordecai. "That's my new motto."

Luba then calls her broker and places the order to transfer just over 25 million dollars to Non-Tom's corporate account. She hands the phone back to Zoey.

"Done," says Luba. "Thank you, Mordecai. I swear I'll be worthy of your trust and pay it back so that you can pay it forward once again when a moment of kindness would come in handy."

After a slight pause, Luba continues.

"I've been thinking. As president of the board of directors and majority stockholder, I am well aware that I need to surround myself with people smarter than me, people I trust. Therefore, as my first official act, I am awarding you both, Lindy and Zoey, my two best friends, two hundred shares of stock in appreciation of your bravery when securing the safety of this company. I'll have the transfer papers drawn up when we get back home."

You Can Call Me Andy

"Way cool," says Zoey. "I didn't see that coming."

"And I can't believe I can say words like that," says Luba. "One more thing. For you, dear *meshugener* crazy canine, since stocks won't do you any good, I will underwrite a lifetime subscription for your application software updates."

Andy bows his head in Luba's direction. They both smile. "Thank you," says the dog.

"Never Conduct Business Without Dark Chocolate," says Luba. "That's my motto."

"Oh, god," says Lindy. "Good thinking, Luba Vilnitsky! But is it possible to get a cocktail with that chocolate?"

"I know where the quality stash is hidden, Miss Lindy," says Mordecai. "Don't go anywhere."

Andy joins Mordecai in the kitchen. As Mordecai pulls bottles out of the liquor cabinet, their talk drifts to the topic of using thought to influence the future, and how to harness that ability.

"I'm thinking… coherent intention combined with consistent effort and focus," says Andy.

"So thought becomes an energy force?" asks Mordecai.

"Exactly," says Andy. "Focused thinking about thinking, guided by benevolence."

"You heard Zoey speak of her joy a moment ago," says Mordecai. "A solar housing project in your home town in Oregon. Money can help a benevolent dream come true. I'd sure like to be part of that dream."

Chapter 16: Not Quite The Ending

The Jew Girls adventure could have ended right there—true love a possibility and big financial rewards looming. But while it's fine to imply happy endings, the Jew Girls still have work to do. It's one thing to dream big innovative ideas for solving the problems of a small coastal town, it's another to take those ideas and transform them into reality.

And what about all those loose ends? What happens to Ozzy, the red-haired rabbi on the Maui commune?

(Luba actually wrote back to thank Ozzy for the Jewish star necklace and she still keeps it in her jewelry box although she never wears it. Soon after returning home to Newport, a letter from him arrived—eight pages double-sided, handwritten in beautiful script. A tender summation of his life's wishes, hopes, and dreams, and how they had changed over time and what they are now. Luba chose not to respond and that was that.)

What about Clint Eastwood and Oprah? What about Kris Kristofferson? Do they get just that one, small, walk-on part at Non-Tom's cocktail party?

(Yes, too bad. But they all really do have homes on Maui, so if the Jew Girls return to visit Non-Tom or Mordecai someday, we might run into them again.)

Did the head honcho from the Florida syndicate or any of their henchmen end up in jail for investment fraud?

(No. Appeals and trial delays are still ongoing. Their lawyers will probably get them off entirely, or at most, they'll be confined to house arrest. Even the judicial system loses when pitted against big money. It's totally unfair.)

Was the blackmail of Elon Musk resolved?

(Yes and no. It's a complicated dark web.)

And let's not forget Senor Zippy, the iguana, left under the care of the housekeeper back in Oregon.

So that's exactly where we pick up the story.

Chapter 17: What Does The Iguana Say?

"Did I ever tell you why my name is Senor Zippy?" asks Senor Zippy in his slow, sleepy voice. Zippy's head is bobbing up and down slowly, a sign that all is well in his world.

"No, you haven't, but I'll take the bait," responds Andy to the pampered iguana. "Tell me, please, why is your name Senor Zippy?"

"Because I hardly ever move and never accomplish anything," chuckles Senor Zippy. "But I'm Luba's therapy companion. We communicate on a numinous level."

The iguana and dog are in Luba's bedroom. As usual, a female rap singer is belting her powerful message across the airwaves. Luba enters the room and approaches her iguana. She sets down a plastic champagne glass next to Senor Zippy. In the glass is a sludge of liquefied vegetables and fruit.

"Your dinner, my sweet Senor Zippy," Luba says to her beloved. Then she heads back outside to sit with her friends on the balcony. The sun will be setting soon.

You Can Call Me Andy

"So, Andy," says Senor Zippy. "How was Hawaii?" Senor Zippy heaves his green body onto an orchid-print toddler-sized lounge chair.

Before Andy has a chance to answer, the iguana says, "Look at me! My mistress brought this chaise lounge back from Hawaii. She did it for *me*! I'm a movie star!"

"May I speak now?" asks Andy.

"Of course," the iguana says; petulance and testiness in his voice.

"We had a wonderful time," says Andy. "Freaky investment people, very few wounds, surprisingly excellent food. I met Willie Nelson. Spent the night with a whippet. There was this mongoose…."

"Who is Willy Nelson?" interrupts the iguana. "Is he a movie star?"

"He's a famous country music singer and songwriter," says Andy. "You know, 'Blue Eyes Crying in the Rain,' 'Angel Flying Too Close To the Ground,' the song 'Crazy' made famous by Patsy Cline? Any of those ring a bell? He's one of my favorites. I'm surprised you've never heard of him."

"I'm partial to my mistress's selections," says the iguana. "Very loud hip-hop. That's all we listen to. Even though it hurts my ears. I love her."

"Have you ever considered…." begins Andy.

"That's enough!" says Senor Zippy. "My turn. Don't I look like a maharajah? Does my color clash with the stripes of the chaise lounge?"

Andy rolls his eyes. "You know what, Zippy," he says. "Seeing your dinner there makes me hungry. They've got snacks on the balcony. If I sit close enough to the deli plate, Zoey will eventually toss me a morsel."

The Jew Girls are in deep discussion and pay no attention when Andy joins them. He never takes for granted Luba's amazing 180-degree view of the Pacific.

"Okay, gals," says Lindy, clinking her bracelets on her glass for attention. "I'm reporting in regarding my assignment to inventory all property of at least one acre available in Newport city limits. I never figured my expired real estate license would ever again come in handy. But you'd be surprised at the doors it still opens." She pauses to sip her vodka soda.

The others wait patiently.

Surprisingly, it's not raining and the early spring sun gives their Hawaiian sun-kissed arms and legs a golden glow. Zoey closes her eyes, the better to soak in the chilly warmth.

"It comes down to only one acceptable parcel," says Lindy. "The ten-acre County Fairgrounds property Zoey keeps talking about. It really is perfect for affordable workforce housing. The property is flat and already has infrastructure connections. It's snuggled between a middle school and high school. Kids could walk to class. It's in the downtown core, which means adults could walk to work."

"One-, two-, and three-bedroom apartments," says Zoey. "A cluster of attractive buildings with balconies that rise three, four, or maybe even five-stories high. Commercial space on the ground floor where there could be a laundromat, a bodega for groceries, a café, a pizza parlor that serves beer, whatever is needed. The storefronts could be businesses owned and run by the residents. With room for a playground, a daycare center, classroom space...."

You Can Call Me Andy

"Wait a minute," says Lindy. She plunges her hands deep into her pockets, but they come up empty. "Oh," she says sheepishly. "For a moment there I forgot I gave up smoking."

"And we'll slap you around if you ever start again," says Luba. "I mean that in the nicest way."

"She's trying to say how pleasant it is not to breathe in second-hand smoke," says Zoey.

Lindy stares at her friends with annoyance.

"Okay, sorry," says Luba. "We're really proud of you, Lindy. Now can we continue? Zoey, keep talking. I like where you're going with this."

"There'd even be enough room for tree-lined, circular walking paths through greenspaces, and fields where kids can play soccer and softball. Anyway, that's my dream," says Zoey. "I'm done. That's the big picture."

"But," says Lindy, "there's one roadblock, and it's huge. The county won't loosen its grip on building a convention center and livestock arena on that land and no public vote is required."

"Zoey, did you ever get the City to agree to buy back the property?" asks Luba.

"The city mucky mucks said it would be possible. Something they would consider," says Zoey. "But I never got that in writing. Somehow I was diverted from the task and ended up in Maui that day."

"Well, we will need the City to buy back that property and change the zoning," adds Lindy. "If the City owned it, the land could be developed into a neighborhood of five hundred apartments. That wouldn't be enough new housing, but it would be a start."

"Or," says Luba dramatically. "We need a private developer with sufficient funds to get the county's attention and convince it to sell. Perhaps we have a serendipitous situation here." Luba actually chuckles.

"I found the deed for when the city sold the property to the county for ten dollars. That was in nineteen thirty-seven," says Lindy. "In case that helps."

"You betcha it does," says Luba. "That document is part of the land's history and should be included when determining financial basis, so yes, absolutely do hold onto it. All we need is an architectural plan, a detailed budget, and lots of money." She grins big at her friends. "What do you say, gals?"

"Let's do it!" says Lindy.

"And just where does the 'lots of money' come from?" asks Zoey.

"The mission of the company I now head includes underwriting solar housing experiments worldwide," says Luba. "I see no reason Newport couldn't be a test site."

"Really? Oh my god! We could fight the county and score one for the people!" shrieks Zoey. "This is so exciting!"

"Let's rephrase," says Luba. "Not fight the county. How about offer the county a financial deal it couldn't refuse?"

"Brilliant!" says Lindy. "What *chutzpah!* A development like that could provide housing for all those nurses, doctors, teachers, scientists, restaurant and hotel workers coming to the coast for jobs," says Lindy. "It would keep them from leaving when they realize there's no place to live."

"It would also encourage high school graduates to remain here when they need to move out of their parent's homes," says Zoey. "If we also built an industrial arts school on the Fairgrounds

You Can Call Me Andy

property, we could teach those kids plumbing and electrical repair, carpentry, welding, auto mechanics...."

"It would trigger an era of prosperity for the residents of the City of Newport!" says Lindy.

"Well, then, my friends, a toast to Newport's future!" says Luba, raising her glass.

"*L'chaim!*" says Zoey.

"*L'chaim!*" says Lindy swallowing the last drop of her drink.

"You never know what's right around the corner," says Andy raising a paw.

"Is that a non-sequitur?" asks Zoey.

"Not at all," says Andy. "It's the truth."

Zoey cocks her head to help understand her mystifying dog, but gives up. She turns to Luba.

"So, Luba," Zoey says, "now that you proved investment fraud, got the imposter arrested, stopped a hostile takeover by a petrochemical syndicate, became head of your favorite solar development company, and are being taken seriously for your knowledge and skills even though you're a woman, does that mean you've settled your personal vendetta and are done with revenge?"

"When Mordecai refused to bow down and Haman vowed to destroy all the Jews in Persia in retaliation, that was revenge," says Luba. "When the Jews mobilized to defend themselves and slaughtered seventy-five thousand of the King's soldiers, and then held a big party to celebrate, that was revenge. Purim is all about revenge. But I've decided I'm not."

"Really?" says Lindy. "Then what do you call what you just pulled off?"

"Justice," says Luba, giving them a dazzling smile.

"Listen," says Lindy looking at her empty glass. "I hate to say it, Luba Vilnitsky, but there is something missing in your drinks. No offense, *darlink*, but it's not nearly as good as the cocktails Mordecai fixed for us. Those were the best whatevers I've ever tasted."

"I kind of wish Mordecai was here, too," says Zoey.

"And not just for his bartending skills," chortles Lindy.

Luba snickers and Zoey blushes.

Just then, there's a loud knock at the apartment's front door.

"Expecting someone?" asks Lindy.

The knock sounds again.

"Is your housekeeper here?" asks Zoey.

When Luba shakes her head no, Zoey says, "I'll get it. I'll say you're not home and send whoever it is away."

That's when things get interesting.

Zoey opens the front door and standing there is Mordecai. He looks like his usual fantastic self, and smells of blooming hibiscus. He has a four-foot cardboard tube tucked under one arm, and holds a shaker of mixed drinks. Zoey's eyes open wide and her body vibrates.

"I knew I was in the right place," says Mordecai. "I heard laughing and looked up and there you were, m'lady, on the balcony. Might I come in?"

Zoey steps aside and Mordecai enters. He walks through the white apartment to the balcony and sets the shaker down next to the deli platter. He takes a seat in an empty chair.

The dog sits on his haunches next to the gentleman. He rests his prominent jaw on Mordecai's knee. Mordecai greets him with a good throat scratching.

"Afternoon, Andy, m'ladies," says Mordecai, grinning as he refills their cocktail glasses. "A toast to the highest and best use of solar for the benefit of the people of Newport, Oregon! *L'chaim!*"

The ladies, in shock, touch glasses with him but can't speak. There's something bewildering about their Maui chauffeur and investment partner showing up on the central coast of Oregon.

"And to you three descendants of ancient Persia who routed out a current-day Haman, thereby saving the kingdom!" he continues.

After a moderately long silence, Luba finally asks, "How the hell did you get here?"

"Commercial airline and a car rental from the Portland airport. I hope I'm not interrupting, my dear Miz Vilnitsky," grins Mordecai. "But we, meaning the board of directors and me, are confident you can take our solar technology and create something great for Newport. And we want to get started right away."

"No. I mean, why are you in Oregon?" asks Luba.

"Your friend, the so-called Non-Tom, and I discussed the idea Zoey raised in Maui."

"What idea?" asks Zoey.

"A possible solution to Newport's housing crisis," says Mordecai. "We've been testing a solar panel system that works well on 4-Plexes and 8-Plexes, but it seems to work at maximum efficiently on roofs of high-density housing projects. That's when we made the connection. Remember back in Maui when Zoey said her joy would be to transform the fairgrounds property into a pedestrian-friendly solar-powered neighborhood?"

The Jew Girls Adventure Series

All three Jew Girls shake their heads no.

"Okay then," says Mordecai. "Well, she did. So Non-Tom and I worked out preliminary plans. We were so excited I decided to deliver them in person. These are the first draft, of course, a starting point for your consideration."

Luba takes the rolled documents and spreads them open on the table.

Lindy sips her drink, her brow furrowed. She needs time to process, so she blurts out, "Since I can't have tobacco, I need another kind of pacifier. Back in a sec." She heads off to Luba's kitchen to find some dark chocolate.

Zoey looks at Mordecai with wonderment. "Who *are* you?" she asks.

"A true believer," says Mordecai. "In solar power, of course. But also in you, Zoey. Listening to you speak is like reading a book I can't put down."

As if an explosion was detonated deep inside her, Zoey feels severed from her logical mind.

Andy moves in and leans all his bodyweight against Zoey. He figures physical connection will help keep her grounded. Zoey puts a hand on the dog's neck. Her fingers grab hold deep in his thick fur. He times his breathing to match hers and then deliberately slows them down.

"Dark chocolate-covered Bing cherries are the perfect complement for cocktails," says Lindy when she returns and sets a bowl of the delectables on the table. "And look who followed me out here."

Senor Zippy climbs Luba's sturdy leg and heaves his way up her torso, settling like a heavy, green muffler around her neck.

You Can Call Me Andy

"An iguana?" asks Mordecai.

"Never mind Senor Zippy," says Luba. "Let's hear your plan."

"Okay," says Mordecai even though he finds the lizard distracting. 'We'll, umm, we'll need to bring in a building contractor experienced in high-density, energy-efficient workforce housing."

"Of course," says Luba impatiently.

"Well, I have someone in mind," says Mordecai. "Myself. Which would mean I'd need to spend quite a bit of time in Newport during the next few months… to get the property title transferred and all the permits signed."

"Oh wow, oh wow!" shrieks Lindy. She looks at her cocktail glass, ready to raise it, but alas, it's empty again. Her right thumb flicks as if she's using a lighter.

"Yes!" says Zoey, hoping her answer stands for even more, even though no question was asked.

"I vote aye, too," says Andy.

"Wait a minute," says Senor Zippy. "If the dog gets a vote, don't iguanas count?"

Senor Zippy has always suffered from FOMO, the Fear of Missing Out. A pout forces his wide mouth into a perplexed downturn, and the rapid side-to-side head bobbing is a sure sign he's upset.

"For the record," he adds, "I'm in favor too, as long as the kids' playground has a sandpit and trees to climb. And a heat lamp for those damp northwestern days. A win-win!" Senor Zippy shouts, dewlaps flaring in excitement. "It's about time you all got woke!"

Mordecai is generally an open-minded man, but the iguana has him stymied. "Just how did you and Senor Zippy meet?" he asks Luba, trying to be tactful.

The Jew Girls Adventure Series

"Oh... that's a long story involving Mexico's Yucatan Peninsula and a Mayan archeologist," says Luba.

Zoey, her mind still reeling, lights a joint to calm down, inhales deeply, and passes it to Lindy, who imbibes and passes it to Luba.

Luba suggests they all head to the bay front for more drinks, dinner, and dancing. "The band there tonight doesn't do rap or hip-hop, but I'm willing to give it a try."

"You are a strange group," Mordecai says to Andy. "Idiosyncratic. Quite appealing. Hard to know what to expect."

"And you're rich," says Andy. "So let's see what kind of benevolent adventure we can whip up. Something to provide hope in this era of national amorality. Maybe we really can harness thought and influence the future."

Luba hands the joint to Mordecai.

"I just want to say," says Luba, "I love you guys. So much!"

"Do you smoke?" Mordecai asks the dog, who shakes his head no.

"I'm a dog," says Andy.

Mordecai examines the joint, then puts it to his lips and inhales.

Luba follows Zoey, Lindy, and Andy indoors. Mordecai slides the balcony door closed behind him.

"I'm so excited, I think I'm gonna scream," says Lindy.

And then she does.

THE END

Appendix A: Yiddish & Hawaiian Words Mentioned In This Story

YIDDISH

A sheynem dank: Thank you very much.

Bubbelah: Endearing term for someone you like, young or old, anyone close to your heart.

Challah: Yeast-leavened, braided sweet bread glazed with an egg mixture to give it a shiny look. Traditionally eaten by Ashkenazi Jews of Eastern European origin on the Sabbath, holidays, and other ceremonial occasions, but never on Passover.

Chutzpah: Audacity, brazenness, gall.

Draikop: One who confuses you; one who connives and twists facts to serve his own purpose.

Dumkop: Idiot, dumbbell, dunce.

Ech!: A groan; a disparaging exclamation.

Goniff: Thief.

Got in himmel!: God in heaven! Usually uttered in anguish, despair, fear, or frustration.

Groisser potz!: A big penis, prick, fool; a big shot.

Gragger: Noisemaker used during the reading of the Megillah. Whenever the name of Haman is mentioned, children swing graggers and make a lot of noise to show contempt for him.

Hamantaschen: Traditional Purim pastry in the shape of Haman's three-cornered hat. Normally filled with poppy seeds, fruit preserves, or prunes.

L'chaim!: A toast—To life!

The Jew Girls Adventure Series

Mazel tov: Good luck! Also, congratulations!

Megillah: The scroll containing the Book of Esther.

Meshugener: Mad, crazy, insane man.

Mezuzah: A tiny piece of parchment inscribed with two Hebrew verses from the Torah, placed inside a decorative case attached to the front door frame—on the right as one enters. The top is slanted towards the house's interior. A mezuzah distinguishes a Jewish home as a visible symbol to all those who enter that Jewish identity and commitment exists inside. It is a reminder that our homes are holy places, and that we should act accordingly—when we enter and when we leave to go out into the world.

Mishegas: insanity, silliness, craziness used in an affectionate way.

Nosh: To eat a snack or light meal.

Nudnik: Obtuse, annoying, boring, bothersome person; a pest.

Oy gevalt: Cry of anguish, suffering, or frustration.

Oy vey: Dear me! Expression of dismay, exasperation, hurt, or woe.

Schlump: Careless, unkempt, sloppy dresser; a jerk.

Verklempt: Overcome with emotion; overwhelmed; flustered; nervous.

Vos iz mit dir?: What's wrong with you?

HAWAIIAN

Kanaka: Native Hawaiian

Mahalo: Thanks, thank you

Okole maluna!: Bottoms up!

Appendix B:
The Story Of Purim

The story of Purim is found in the Old Testament Book of Esther and takes place in Ancient Persia in the fourth century BCE. Three years after arrogant King Ahasuerus ascended the throne he held a celebration to flaunt his power by throwing a party that lasted 180 days. He then hosted a weeklong party for just the male residents of his city. On the final day of the party, Ahasuerus commanded his wife, Queen Vashti, to appear. He wanted to show off her exquisite beauty to the drunken revelers. Vashti refused, so Ahasuerus had her executed. But, as so often happens with men, the king soon became lonely for a wife. To remedy the situation, he decreed that a beauty pageant would be held and the most beautiful woman would become his new queen. Esther, who had no desire to be queen, was forcibly taken from her home and lined up as one of the contestants. When the king chose her, she wanted to refuse, but Mordecai, the uncle who adopted her when her parents died, advised her to keep her mouth shut, become queen, and never divulge that she was a Jew. The king was no friend to Jews.

Shortly after, Mordecai overheard two of the palace guards discussing a plot to assassinate King Ahasuerus. He reported the incident to the king and the traitors were hanged. Meanwhile, Haman, one of the king's ministers and a well-known Jew hater, was promoted to the position of prime minister. The king issued a decree ordering everyone to bow down whenever Haman walked by. When Mordecai refused (he was a proud Jew), Haman vowed revenge against him.

Mordecai prayed for a solution, but Esther strategized a plan. She asked Mordecai to gather all the Jews in the capital city and have them fast with her for three days and nights. When the fast was over, Esther entered Ahasuerus' chambers. Amazingly, he didn't order her immediate

The Jew Girls Adventure Series

execution (which was the punishment for approaching the king without first being summoned). When he asked what she wanted, she invited him, and Haman, to feast with her. During the meal, the king asked Esther if she had any requests. "Yes," she responded. "I invite the king and Haman to join me for another feast tomorrow. At that time I will tell the king my request."

Haman left the first feast a happy and proud man. Oh, the honor he was being accorded! But standing at the king's gate was Mordecai, who still refused to bow to him, and Haman again vowed revenge. When he arrived home, his wife and wise advisers counseled him to erect a gallows and ask the king for permission to hang Mordecai. This idea excited Haman greatly, and he went out and erected the gallows right away. He was so smitten with his plan that he decided to eradicate all the Jews in Persia on one single day. He chose the 13th day of the month of Adar as the fateful day by casting lots (the Hebrew word for lots is "purim"). He asked for, and received permission from the king.

Meanwhile, King Ahasuerus was told of a brave Jew named Mordecai who had saved the king's life by reporting a murder plot. The king asked, "Was this man rewarded for his fine act?" "No, he was not," the king was told. At that very moment, Haman entered the king's courtyard and King Ahasuerus asked, "Haman, in your estimation, what shall be done to a person whom the king wishes to honor?" Haman, certain he was the man the king wished to honor, responded that he should dress the man in royal purple robes, put him on a white horse, and parade him through town. "Make it so," the king said. "That is what we will do for Mordecai." Haman had no choice but to comply.

The next day, Haman joined the king and Esther for the second feast. When the king asked Esther to name her request, she first dropped the bombshell that she was a Jew. Then she said, "There's a bad man who wishes to kill Mordecai, the man you just honored, as well as me, and all our people." The king asked, "Who is this evil man?" Esther replied, "That man!" she said, pointing to Haman. She said Haman had already erected a gallows to hang Mordecai. This angered the king, so he ordered that Haman be hanged on his own gallows.

Done! Haman was dead, but his evil decree to kill all the Jews in Persia in one single day was still in effect. (Once a king issued a decree, it could not be rescinded.) At Esther's request, the king wrote another decree that granted the Jews permission to defend themselves against their enemies. On the 13th day of Adar, the Jews throughout the Persian Empire mobilized and killed the enemies who had intended to kill them. Among the 75,000 dead were Haman's ten sons. Ah, joyous revenge! Esther then asked the king to allow the Jews one more day to kill the rest of their enemies in the capital city, and Ahasuerus agreed. On that day, they hung Haman's ten sons, even though the men had already perished in battle. Then the Jews rested, and the next day, they partied.

Purim, celebrated on the 14th of Adar each year, is the most joyous holiday on the Jewish calendar. The point is, even in the face of danger and fear, we should celebrate surviving another day.

In modern times, to commemorate Purim, we fast from dawn to dusk in solidarity with Esther's three-day fast as she prepared to face the king. And then we hold the Big Megillah Party ("Megillah" refers to the handwritten, parchment Scroll of Esther). At the party, costumes representing Esther, Mordecai, and Haman are encouraged and the Megillah is chanted out loud. During the reading, kids spin noisemakers (graggers and air horns), and yell "boo!" every time the name Haman is mentioned. Adults and kids can also write the name Haman on the bottom of their shoes and stamp their feet to eradicate his evil name. The point of the party is to get so drunk that we can't tell the difference between Haman and Mordecai.

Purim celebrates the idea that the Jews could take such a potentially horrible event and turn it into a celebration of strength, perseverance, and community.

Appendix C:
Hamantaschen Pastry Recipe

Hamantaschen (plural for hamantash) are traditionally eaten during Purim. These triangle-shaped pastries are filled with poppy seeds, fruit preserves, or mashed prunes. In Yiddish, hamantaschen means Haman's hat. Or Haman's pocket ("tash"). Or Haman's ears.

Ingredients (makes about 35 pastries)

4 large eggs
1 cup sugar
1/2 cup canola oil
1 lemon (juice and zest)
1 tsp. pure vanilla extract
5 cups flour, plus more for dusting
2 tsp. baking powder
1/2 tsp. salt
1-1/2 cups poppy seed filling (see below)—or thick fruit preserves such as apricot or strawberry—or mashed prunes

Instructions

In a large bowl, combine eggs and sugar. Whisk until light and foamy. Add oil, lemon juice and zest, and vanilla extract. Combine flour, baking powder, and salt. Use a wooden spoon or stiff rubber spatula to add dry ingredients to the egg mixture. Stir well until a stiff dough forms. Shape into three balls. Wrap each ball in waxed paper and refrigerate 4 hours (or overnight). Meanwhile, prepare the filling.

Poppy seed filling

1 cup poppy seeds	Pinch of salt
Boiling water, enough to cover seeds	1/2 cup water
2 tablespoons sugar	1/2 cup finely chopped
1/4 cup honey	almonds

You Can Call Me Andy

Pour boiling water over poppy seeds and let stand until cool; drain. Pound seeds well (or use a coffee grinder). Cook poppy seeds with sugar, honey, salt, and water over moderate heat until thick, stirring frequently. Remove from heat and stir in chopped almonds. Let cool.

When dough is ready, lightly flour a clean work surface. Remove one ball at a time from the refrigerator. Grease the baking sheets.

Using a rolling pin, roll out dough to 1/6-inch thick. Use a 3¾-inch round cookie cutter or the rim of a glass to cut circles in the dough. Pull the scraps away from the circles and set aside to be re-rolled into additional circles. Place 1/2 teaspoon of poppy seed mix (or fruit preserve) in the center of each circle.

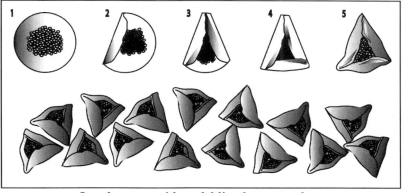

Step-by-step guide to folding hamantaschen

To create the triangle shape, fold in three sides. Pinch the dough closed at the corners to seal, but leave a small opening in the center top. If a corner won't seal, dip a finger in water then touch the corner and pinch again. Place triangles an inch apart on baking sheets. Repeat process with remaining balls of dough. Chill the baking sheets for 30 minutes before placing in oven. Preheat oven to 350°F.

Bake the cookies until golden brown, 10 to 15 minutes. Remove and let the pastries cool on the baking sheets for 1 minute, then transfer to wire racks to cool completely.

Appendix D:
Real Musicians Mentioned In This Story

Megan Thee Stallion *(song referenced in Chapter 2)*

Megan Jovon Ruth Pete (born February 15, 1995 in Houston, Texas), known professionally as Megan Thee Stallion, is an American rapper, singer, and songwriter. "Pimpin'," was released on her album *Fever* in May 2019. In 2020, *Time* magazine named her one of the 100 most influential people in the world. She was also featured on Saturday Night Live demanding justice for Breonna Taylor, a 26-year-old who was fatally shot in her Louisville, Kentucky, apartment on March 13, 2020 by white plainclothes officers investigating drug dealing that had nothing to do with her. In November 2020, she released her album, *Good News*, and published *Why I Speak Up For Black Women*, an op-ed in the *New York Times*. In March 2021, she won Grammys for best New Artist, Best Rap Song, and Best Rap Performance. https://megantheestallion.com/; https://genius.com/Megan-thee-stallion-pimpin-lyrics
Op Ed piece: https://www.nytimes.com/2020/10/13/opinion/megan-thee-stallion-black-women.html

Lizzo *(song referenced in Chapter 2)*

Melissa Viviane Jefferson (born April 27, 1988), known professionally as Lizzo, is an American singer, rapper, songwriter, and flutist. Born in Detroit, Michigan, she attained mainstream success with the release of her third studio album, *Cuz I Love You* (2019). The album spawned the single: "Juice," (see Chapter 2 of this story). Lizzo received eight nominations at the 62nd Annual Grammy Awards, the most for any artist in 2020. She won the awards for Best Urban Contemporary Album, Best Pop Solo Performance, and Best Traditional R&B Performance. Lizzo is also an actor. In 2019, *Time* named her Entertainer of the Year for her meteoric rise and contribution to music. She's also won a *Billboard* Music Award, a BET Award, and two Soul Train Music Awards. https://www.lizzomusic.com; https://www.blameitonmyjuice.com/

You Can Call Me Andy

Bill Withers *(song referenced in Chapter 2)*

Bill Withers Jr. (July 4, 1938-March 30, 2020) was born in Slab Fork, West Virginia, a town of 200 people. He was an American singer-songwriter and musician with hits that included "Ain't No Sunshine" (1971), "Grandma's Hands" (1971), "Use Me" (1972), "Lean on Me" (1972), "Lovely Day" (1977), and "Just the Two of Us" (1981). He won three Grammy Awards and was nominated for six more. His life was the subject of the 2009 documentary film *Still Bill*. Withers was inducted into the Songwriters Hall of Fame in 2005 and the Rock and Roll Hall of Fame in 2015. https://billwithers.com/

Roy Orbison *(song referenced in Chapter 7)*

Roy Orbison (1936-1988) was born in Vernon, Texas, and was a musician and singer/songwriter of rock, pop, country, and rock & roll. He played guitar and harmonica solo as well as with The Traveling Wilburys (Bob Dylan, George Harrison, Tom Petty, and Jeff Lynne). He also sang with k.d. lang, Bruce Springsteen, Emmylou Harris, Johnny Cash, Jerry Lee Lewis, Carl Perkins, Waylon Jennings, and Jessi Colter. Orbison's honors include inductions into the Rock and Roll Hall of Fame and Nashville Songwriters Hall of Fame in 1987, the Songwriters Hall of Fame in 1989, and the Musicians Hall of Fame and Museum in 2014. He received a Grammy Lifetime Achievement Award and five other Grammy Awards. *Rolling Stone* placed him at number 37 on its list of the "Greatest Artists of All Time" and number 13 on its list of the "100 Greatest Singers of All Time." He toured the world for decades, and in 1963, performed sold-out concerts in Australia and New Zealand with The Beach Boys and then with the Rolling Stones. That same year, he recorded the song, "Oh, Pretty Woman." https://royorbison.com/

Maccabeats *(song referenced in Chapter 8)*

The Maccabeats are an American Orthodox Jewish all-male a cappella group. Founded in 2007 at Yeshiva University in Manhattan, the 14-member group specializes in covers and parodies of contemporary hits using Jewish themes. Their breakout 2010 Hanukkah music video for "Candlelight" logged more than two million hits in its first ten days.

The Jew Girls Adventure Series

They have recorded three albums and one EP, and frequently release music videos in conjunction with Jewish holidays. They tour worldwide and have performed at the White House and the Knesset. Their albums include *Voices from the Heights* (2010), *Out of the Box* (2012), and *One Day More* (2014). http://www.maccabeats.com/.
Maccabeats singing Purim song: https://youtu.be/2EDBvtMLntI

Jimmy LaFave (*song referenced in Chapter 9*)

Jimmy LaFave was an American singer-songwriter and folk musician born in Texas in 1955. After moving to Stillwater, Oklahoma, he helped develop what became known as Red Dirt Music. Always a great admirer of Woody Guthrie, LaFave joined the Advisory Board and became a regular performer at the annual Woody Guthrie Folk Festival. In 1996, LaFave received the Kerrville Folk Festival songwriter of the year award and appeared on the TV show *Austin City Limits* for the first time. Over his career, he recorded 15 albums of his own and wrote a number of songs made famous by others. He died on May 21, 2017 from a rare form of cancer and was posthumously inducted into the Oklahoma Music Hall of Fame in 2017, as well as officially recognized by the Governor of Texas for his songwriting contributions to the Texas music scene. The song, "Car Outside," was included on the album *Cimarron Manifesto*, released in 2007. https://jimmylafave.com/

Lady Gaga (*song referenced in Chapter 9*)

Stefani Joanne Angelina Germanotta, born in 1986, is known professionally as Lady Gaga. She is an American singer, songwriter, and actress notorious for her image reinventions and musical versatility. In 2008, she rose to prominence with her debut studio album, *The Fame*, and its chart-topping singles "Just Dance" and "Poker Face." The album was reissued in 2009 to include *The Fame Monster*, which yielded the extremely successful single, "Bad Romance." http://ladygaga.com; https://youtu.be/qrO4YZeyl0I

About The Authors

JESS BONDY traces her family roots to Russian and Eastern European Jews who emigrated to the Lower East Side of Manhattan in the late 1800s. Although she grew up next to a synagogue, her family belonged to The New York Society for Ethical Culture.

DNA tests reveal Jess is 99.9 percent Ashkenazi Jew. While not raised religiously, she feels a strong connection to her cultural heritage. Jess self-identifies as a food Jew. She developed her love of cooking from her mother, who passed down family recipes Jess prepares to this day. Jess took creative liberties in resurrecting her beloved mother Lindy as the character bearing that name in this book series.

Jess relocated to the Pacific Northwest, earning a B.S. in Anthropology and a Masters in Urban and Regional Planning from the University of Oregon. Her early jobs took her to the Cascade Mountains and the high desert. She also spent years as an archaeologist working on digs and surveys throughout the state of Oregon. Jess retired after a career working 30+-years as Senior Planner for the Lincoln County Department of Planning and Development based in Newport, Oregon. Jess and her spouse live a quiet, rural life on the Central Oregon Coast with their cats and dogs.

SARA LOU HEIMLICH was born into a non-religious but somewhat cultural Jewish family. Her own Jewish identity has been developing for more than 40 years. Her fondest memories of her Ukrainian immigrant maternal grandmother include the Passover and Hanukkah feasts she would prepare, always insisting, "Eat, eat, darlings, eat!"

Sara Lou has two sisters, yet she is the only one with a middle name. Family lore is that "Lou" honors Luba, her Russian great-grandmother (left behind when her son—Sara Lou's maternal grandfather—stowed

The Jew Girls Adventure Series

away on a ship traveling from Russia to the USA using his brother's passport), and Lucien, a Swiss professor who was monumental in her parents' growth as physicians after World War II. Either name would have stopped people who always ask her where she's from in the South.

Sara Lou has a B.A. in Art and Biology and a Master's in Marine Sciences. She worked for 30+ years as a whale biologist and freelance graphic artist. A well-seasoned writer of academic papers and popular science articles, the Jew Girl Adventure Series Book One: *You Can Call Me Andy*, is Sara Lou's first venture into pure storytelling.

CARLA PERRY graduated from the University of Iowa's Writers Workshop with a degree in Creative Writing/Poetry; was founder and volunteer director of Writers On The Edge and Nye Beach Writers' Series, which hosted monthly events year-round for 20 years; is author of a few published books of poetry, and *Riva Beside Me,* a novel that was transformed into a full stage play. She received an Oregon Literary Arts Fellowship in Fiction, a Career Opportunity Grant from the Oregon Arts Commission, and several writing residencies. Her poetry, essays, interviews, short stories, and photos of other writers have been published widely. She also received the Stewart Holbrook Special Oregon Book Award and the Oregon Governor's Art Award.

Carla co-wrote and published the literary magazine *Wild Dog* while living in a 1976 Chevy campervan for almost five years, and is the founding editor and publisher of *Talus & Scree International Literary Journal*. After 22 years as owner Dancing Moon Press, she retired in 2018. In 2022, she received the Soapstone's Bread & Roses Award, which honors a woman whose work has sustained the writing community.

Carla's ancestors were all Jews, some Orthodox, living in the Bronx and Brooklyn. After decades of not thinking about it, she began honoring her Jewish blood after the Jew Girls began meeting at her house for Passover and Hanukkah celebrations. She has one son, two granddaughters, and a big black dog that looks like a wolf.

You Can Call Me Andy

THE REAL ANDY THE DOG

ANDY was adopted from the Portland Humane Society in 1982 when he was four months old. He lived in Portland, then in Yamhill County at a donkey and goat farm before beginning his cross-country travels with his human companion. In 1990, he left in a 1976 Chevy campervan and spent the next few years circumnavigating the United States, eventually resettling in Oregon along the Siuslaw River. His final move was to Yachats, where he lived for two years prior to his final nap in the sun.

Andy was famous among the denizens of Portland and Central Oregon Coast literary circles, and featured on the covers of magazines and a postcard series. His portrait appeared on the infamous *Wild Dog* T-shirt. Several books were dedicated to him. His hobbies were long-distance walking, getting stroked by strangers, and chasing cats that ran. He was wise, gentle, and always dignified. Andy was an exceptionally good dog.

*Stay tuned for the next exciting Jew Girls Adventure!
If you wish to be notified of upcoming readings
and new book releases
send an email to:
BubbelahPress@gmail.com*